BEAUTY & HER BILLIONAIRE BOSS

BEAUTY & HER BILLIONAIRE BOSS

BY

BARBARA WALLACE

MILLS & BOON

First published in Great Britain 2015
by Mills & Boon, an imprint of Harlequin (UK) Limited,
Large Print edition 2016
Eton House, 18-24 Paradise Road,
Richmond, Surrey, TW9 1SR

© 2015 Barbara Wallace

ISBN: 978-0-263-26149-3

Printed and bound in Great Britain
by CPI Antony Rowe, Chippenham, Wiltshire

To Pete—
your patience and support are a gift for
which I can never say thank you enough.

And to M.G.—for giving someone that dose
of common sense when we most needed it.

CHAPTER ONE

THERE SHOULD BE a law against a man looking so good in a tuxedo. Staring at the man asleep in the chair, Piper felt an appreciative shiver. Monsieur Frederic Lafontaine had shed his jacket and untied his tie, yet he still looked like a million dollars, what with the way his shirt pulled taut across his linebacker-sized shoulders. She had to start using his dry cleaner. The guy must have been sprawled here for hours, and yet his clothes didn't have a single wrinkle. Piper's uniform wouldn't last five minutes. In fact—she ran a hand down the front of her black skirt—it hadn't.

Then again, she didn't have cheekbones that could cut glass or thick brown hair that begged to be touched, either. Maybe perfection came in bundles.

Taking a deep breath, she touched his shoulder and tried not to think about the broad muscles beneath her fingers. Eight months of working for the man, and she still hadn't shaken her attraction. "Monsieur? You need to wake up. It's after seven o'clock."

When he didn't respond, she shook his shoulder again, this time a little more aggressively. The motion did the trick. Slowly, his eyes opened, and he blinked unseeingly. "You fell asleep in the chair," she told him.

"Oh." His voice was thick with sleep, making it deeper and rougher than usual. "What—what time is it?"

"Seven fifteen."

"What?" He bolted to his feet, arms akimbo, his right hand connecting with the cup of coffee Piper set on the end table only seconds before. The cup took flight, sending coffee over everything.

"Dammit!" he hollered as the hot liquid splashed his shirt. He immediately started pulling at the cloth, lifting it from his skin. "How many times have I told you, you must tell me when you put something within reach? You know I can't see anything put to the side."

It was hard to say much of anything seeing as how he jumped up before she had a chance to open her mouth. "I'll get you a towel."

"Don't bother." He'd already yanked the shirt free from his waistband. "Clean up the rest of the spill before it stains the carpet. I'm going to take a shower." He turned to head upstairs.

"Wait," Piper called.

Moving this time before he could speak, she scooped up the cup from where it had fallen on the carpet, half an inch from the toe of his shoe. "You were going to crush it," she said, holding the china teacup in front of his face.

If he appreciated her heads-up behavior, he didn't say so. "Tell Michel when he arrives that I will be ready shortly. And make sure my brief-case is by the front door. *On the left*," he added with emphasis.

As if she would leave it somewhere else. Piper bit back the sarcastic response. She learned a long time ago that some fights weren't meant to be won. Arguing with a man who was wearing hot coffee on his stomach was definitely one of those fights. Instead, she waited until he'd stalked his way upstairs, then treated herself to a glare in his direction. It would serve him right if she moved his bag to the right just to spite him. Because goodness knows the world might end if the briefcase was on the wrong side of the doorway.

Not that she would actually move the thing. Put out or not, she wasn't so petty that she'd pick on a blind man—or half-blind man as the case may be. Truth was, nitpicky as they were, monsieur's "rules" served a purpose. When she took this job, it was made very clear his limited field of vision required everything in the house to be just so. Chief on the list was that nothing should be set to the side without his knowledge. His lack of peripheral vision might cause a mishap, he'd explained. Most of the time, the system worked.

There were times in fact, such as when he crossed the room with his slow, purposeful strides, that Piper forgot the man had trouble seeing.

After double-checking on the briefcase—which was on the left as always—she headed for the utility closet. "So goes another fun-filled day in Paris," she said as she marched into the kitchen for her cleaning supplies. Naturally, the coffee had fallen on the handmade Persian carpet. That meant instead of using the nice handy carpet-cleaning machine in the closet, she had to get the stain up with water and a vinegar paste.

This was not how she expected her year abroad to go. Her year here was supposed to signal the start of a new and exciting life. The wonderful moment when she stopped being dumpy Piper Rush and became Piper Rush, chef extraordinaire who dazzled the culinary institute with her skills and enthralled French men with her American wit. In short, the complete opposite of her life in East Boston.

She should have known better.

Didn't take long for her to realize that Paris was exactly the same as Boston, only in French. Which actually made it worse than Boston. Despite spending hours shoulder to shoulder with a dozen other people, she hadn't made a single close friend. Everyone was too busy trying to impress Chef Despelteau. In a way, you'd think the fact that she couldn't impress the man if she tried would help her cause, but no. Yesterday, after she didn't use enough confit to brown her chicken, he declared her cassoulet flavorless and spent ten minutes lecturing her on the importance of taste, even when making "peasant food." All her classmates did was snicker. City of Lights, her foot. More like the City of the Unfriendly.

Even Frederic barely paid attention to her, unless there was an errand to run, or she needed to wake him up. He was too busy lecturing at the university or heading off to some fancy social event.

The perpetual loneliness she fought to keep under wraps threatened to wedge free. She had to swallow to keep it from rising up and choking her. God, what she wouldn't give for someone to talk to. *Or to go home.*

Out of habit, her hand reached for the cell phone tucked in her apron only to leave it behind. It was still the middle of the night in Boston. Her sister, Patience, would still be asleep. Patience—the only reason she was sticking things out to completion. Her sister was convinced Piper was living the dream, and considering how much Patience had sacrificed so Piper could actually have a dream, she didn't dare disturb the fantasy. Besides, her sister had issues of her own. She and her boss's nephew were doing some kind of back-and-forth that had Patience on edge. The last thing she needed right now was a whiny baby sister burning up the data package complaining because her year abroad wasn't all sunshine and roses.

She carried her supplies into the salon, pausing when she reached the front window. A few blocks away, the Eiffel Tower loomed tall, reminding her she really had no right complaining. She might be lonely, but she was a lonely person living in luxury. Instead of monsieur's mansion, she could be living in some ratty apartment battling roaches for breakfast. Or worse, living on the streets. Been there, done both. She didn't feel like doing either again.

If only she had someone to share Paris with, then things wouldn't be so bad. It wasn't going to happen, though. If she hadn't found a kindred spirit yet, she wasn't going to. She was simply going to have to suck things up, the way she always did.

Speaking of sucking, she had a carpet to clean. Staring at the stain darkening the beige carpet, she sighed. This better not be a sign of how the rest of her day was going to go.

Frederic winced as he peeled the wet shirt from his body. Not because the liquid stung his skin, although it did, but because he was appalled at his behavior. Yelling at his housekeeper that way.

Like a child throwing a tantrum. Didn't he swear he would never be that way? Become one of those angry invalids who took their bad moods out on others? Yet the first time he spills a drink, he lashes out. Embarrassment was no excuse.

What did he expect, falling asleep in the salon like that? It was the last glass of Bordeaux. Knowing the way alcohol went to his head and made him overly pensive, he never should have indulged. Last night found him sitting for hours, watching the tower's twinkling lights, his mind a sea of morose thoughts.

The dampness from his shirt found its way to his palms. Resisting the urge to hurl the garment across the room, he draped it on top of the duvet for Piper to find later. He stripped off the rest of his tuxedo as well, making sure he returned the suit and his shoes to their assigned places in the closet. Oh, but for those days when undressing meant toeing off your shoes wherever you stood and tossing your clothes in a heap.

Obviously, last night's moroseness hadn't subsided. Why else would he be bemoaning a past that he couldn't get back? After all, he'd come to terms with his failing eyesight long before it started to steal his peripheral vision. From the moment the doctors first told him his retina was degenerating, in fact. He knew full well that one day the tunnel through which he viewed the world would close completely, leaving him blind. He'd accepted his fate and framed his life in anticipation. And when the time came, he would shoulder the burden alone, the way a person should. He wouldn't drag others down with him. A promise that, until this morning, he'd done a very good job of keeping.

He owed his housekeeper a very large apology.

When the employment agency first recommended the American culinary student, he thought the idea ridiculous. A temporary resident? She'd be too distracted by studies and sightseeing. But as it turned out, Piper was nothing short of exemplary. Today aside, she did her job quietly and unobtrusively. In fact, the two of them could go days without crossing paths. Precisely the kind of help Frederic preferred.

Today's mistake with the coffee was as much his fault as hers. She no doubt set down the cup to wake him, not expecting him to stand up so quickly.

He would definitely apologize.

Unfortunately, there wasn't time right now. Leaning in close, he read the time on his nightstand clock. With luck, he could shower and make his first class in plenty of time. Whether or not his morning began poorly didn't matter to his superiors at the university. They expected him to deliver his lectures on time, regardless. This evening, then. Before the symphony. He would find Piper and explain that he overreacted. Then they would both forget this morning ever happened.

Staining the carpet turned out to be the high point of the day.

First, cleaning the rug took longer than planned. In addition to the major stain, there were a dozen or so tiny spots that needed blotting. It took her forever to find them all, so by the time Piper finished, she was running late. Chef Despelteau was less than thrilled to see her slip through the door five minutes into his lecture.

Now this.

"Uninspired," Chef Despelteau pronounced. "Your spices, they do not dance, they plod. I expect my students to produce magic in the kitchen, not..." He dropped his fork back onto the plate with an expression that was usually reserved for walking around landfills. Shaking his head, he moved on, his silence letting everyone know Piper wasn't worth more of his time.

"...so pathetic. Why is she even here?"

The whispered comment drifted from the stovetop across the aisle. Apparently whoever said it didn't care if anyone heard him. Why should he, when the whole class was thinking the same thing?

Keeping her shoulders square, Piper stared straight ahead and pretended she didn't hear a thing. That was the number one rule. Never let them think they were getting to you. Never lose control. Never let them see you cry. Crying only gave the bullies power. Let them whisper behind her back all they wanted; she would not give them the satisfaction of seeing so much as a twitch.

She succeeded, too. All through Chef Despelteau's final remarks, through the Métro ride home, and even into the house. She managed to last until she saw the living room carpet and the faint brown ring reminding her she'd failed that task, too. Letting out the coarsest obscenity she knew, she broke down.

Screw cooking school. Tossing her bag in the chair, she stomped into the kitchen. Screw monsieur, too. Him and his impossible-to-clean carpeting. Screw Paris with its beautiful buildings and sidewalk cafés and shops she couldn't afford. She hated them all.

Carbs. She needed carbs. Yanking open the refrigerator door, she grabbed a wedge of cheddar cheese and an onion. Creamy, gooey macaroni and cheese, that's what this pity party needed. *How's that for peasant food, Chef Despelteau?*

Now if she would only stop crying. Sniffing back a fresh batch of tears, she grabbed the cheese grater and took to demolishing the cheddar to a shredded pulp.

"There you—"

"What now?" she snarled. What else could she add to her list of mistakes today?

Frederic blinked in shock. Great. Yelling at her boss. That's what she could add. Because, of course.

Horrified, she turned back to the cheese. "I mean, about this mor—morn..." The tears were back. She scrunched her face trying to stop them.

A paper towel floated in front of her face.

"Is everything all right?"

Why'd he have to sound nice, too? It made things worse. "Fine." Taking the paper towel, she wiped her cheeks and blew her nose.

"You don't look fine."

"The cheese is making my eyes water."

"I see. It must be quite pungent."

Piper ignored the comment, choosing to wipe her nose again instead. "Did you need something, monsieur?"

A tentative smile worked its way across his features. Afraid to set her off again, probably. "I wanted to apologize for losing my temper this morning. The coffee, it was not your fault."

No, it wasn't, she wanted to say. She didn't. Since he apologized, the least she could do was be gracious in return. "I should have known better than to put a cup where you couldn't see it."

"And I should know better than to behave like a brat," he countered, one-upping her. "It's rude to blame others for my shortcomings."

Piper wasn't sure she'd call partial blindness a shortcoming, but she accepted the apology anyway. If she didn't, the two of them might spend all night exchanging regrets. "Thank you," she said with a sniff. The man would never know that his "I'm sorry" had just beat out the coffee stain as the day's bright spot.

"Do you need another paper towel? I would offer you something nicer, but I'm not a hand-kerchief person. A napkin perhaps?"

That made her smile, picturing him retriev-ing a napkin from the linen closet. "Thanks, but I'm okay now." There remained a slight pressure behind her eyes trying to push out tears, but she could keep that under control. A quick splash of water and she'd be fine.

"Are—" She took one last swipe at her nose. "Are you in for the evening?" As if she didn't already know the answer. Frederic was seldom "in." His evenings were one big social engage-ment. How one person could squeeze so much activity into a week, she didn't know.

Just as she expected, Frederic shook his head. "I have tickets for the symphony. I came home to change my shirt is all."

Meaning he would be home late, as usual. "I'll

make sure to leave the foyer light on before I turn in."

"Thank you." He turned to leave only to pause. "Why don't you take the evening off as well? Some time with friends might make you feel better."

Sure it would, if she had friends to go out with. "I…" Thankfully, the *beep* of an incoming message on her cell phone saved her from having to make up some embarrassing lie.

"Sounds like your friends have the same idea," Frederic said.

She reached into her pocket, smiling when she read the message on her screen. "It's my sister," she told him. Why she felt she needed to tell him that, she didn't know.

"You have a sister."

A question as much as a statement. Surely he knew. Then again, he might not. This was the longest conversation they'd ever had.

"She works as a housekeeper back in Boston."

"Ah, so cleaning is a family business."

"More like a family situation we both fell into." From his expression, she could tell he didn't get the joke. No surprise. It wasn't very clear, or funny. "She wants to video chat."

"Sounds like you've got something to look forward to."

"Yeah." Piper smiled. Talking to Patience would definitely make her feel better.

"I'm glad." And for the first time she could remember, he gave her a warm, genuine smile. "I'll leave you alone so you can talk. Good night."

"Good night." To her horror, she almost said "Don't go" instead. Her loneliness was out of control if a smile could make her slip up like that.

Piper waited until she heard the front door shut before going to get her computer. Her apartment sat at the back of the house. Technically, it was more like a suite of rooms—bedroom, bathroom and sitting room—but they were still nicer than anything she could afford on her own. They also came with kitchen privileges and monsieur's kitchen was a dream come true even for an *uninspired* cook like her.

It was into the kitchen that Piper carried her laptop. Patience specifically said video chat, which meant she was planning on a nice long conversation. By putting the laptop on the counter, Piper could cook while they talked. It would be almost like home.

Almost.

A few keystrokes later, Patience Rush's face appeared on screen. Took the older woman about two seconds to frown. "Your eyes are all red and puffy," she said. "Is everything okay?"

Wow, was that the question of the night or what? Maybe she should have looked in a mirror to see how awful she actually looked. "I was chopping onions," Piper replied. At least it was more believable than blaming the cheese.

Too bad her sister didn't let the lie slide as easily as her boss had. "Onions, huh? You sure?"

"Yes, I'm sure."

Patience arched a brow. Her form of mother guilt. It worked every time.

"Okay," Piper admitted, "*maybe* I was thinking about home a little bit too."

"Oh, sweetie, I miss you, too. But hey, a couple more months and you'll be back in Boston bragging to everyone you know how you're a fancy French chef. Do you have any idea how proud I am of you?"

"I do," Piper replied, the familiar knot starting to twist in her stomach. She got the heavy unsettled feeling every time Patience started gushing about her great Paris adventure.

"So what is it that has you video chatting me in the middle of your day?" she asked, changing the topic. Her sister seemed especially bubbly today. A big difference from the last few phone calls. Her image on the screen glowed and not from computer glare either.

"What? A girl can't miss her baby sister?"

"A girl can definitely miss her baby sister." Same way the baby sister could miss her. Piper blinked back some fresh tears. "But usually you text. I know you've got a lot on your plate."

"Never too much for you."

"Awww." Sweet as the sentiment was, Piper wasn't buying. Not with the way her sister's eyes were sparkling. "Seriously, what do you want?"

"I have a favor to ask."

"I knew you wanted something." Although what kind of favor could Piper do from halfway around the world? Send someone a souvenir? "What do you need?"

"I need you to pay a visit to someone there in Paris."

"Who?"

Piper listened as her sister explained. The favor was for Piper to visit the sister of a dead artist named Nigel Rougeau.

"Hey, isn't your boss's cat named Nigel?" she interrupted. Patience was always telling stories about the big Maine coon cat.

"The cat's a namesake," Patience replied.

"Nigel was Ana's lover in the seventies." Ana being the little old lady Patience worked for.

Her sister went on to explain a very tragic story involving Ana and the painter. "There's a small chance that one of the paintings Ana posed for still exists," she said.

"And you want me to talk with Nigel's sister and find out for you."

"If anyone knows if one of Nigel's paintings survived, it would be someone in his family."

True enough. Especially if Nigel and his sister were as close as she and Patience were.

"I think she'd find talking to you a lot less intimidating than a private detective."

"I am definitely unintimidating," Piper replied. More often than not, she was the one intimidated.

"So you'll do it?"

"Of course." A couple hours of her time was nothing. In fact, it would break up the monotony. "I'll call her tomorrow and see if she'll meet with me. Maybe you'll luck out and there'll be a big old painting of Ana hanging in her house."

"Wouldn't that be something," Patience said with a laugh. "Stuart and I will be glad for any information you can find out."

"Stuart, huh?" That was a new development. Until recently, Patience's descriptions of Stuart Duchenko leaned more toward the suspicious jerk variety. Putting down her knife, she leaned close to the screen. "How are things going with the two of you? Is he still cool with, you know, the club?"

"Seems to be," Patience replied.

"See? I told you he'd understand. It's not like you went to work in that place because you liked dancing naked on tables." It was the same reasoning Piper used on herself whenever the teasing at school got to be too much to bear. Of course, she never told Patience about what the kids used to say. Her sister was embarrassed enough.

Case in point, the wince crossing Patience's face right now. "Of course I didn't, and you were right. Stuart says he understands."

"Wait—what do you mean 'says he understands'? Don't you believe him?" There was a note of reluctance in the comment Piper didn't like.

"No, I believe him. Stuart's been great."

"Then what's wrong?"

"Nothing." Patience shook her head.

Nothing came with a very dreamy sigh. No way was Piper letting the reaction go by unnoticed. "Patience? What aren't you telling me?"

"Um…"

Son of a gun, her sister was red as a tomato. There was only one thing that would make her blush that deeply. "Oh my God! Is something going on between you and your boss?"

"He's not my boss," Patience said quickly. "He's my boss's nephew."

She was splitting hairs and they both knew it, which was why Piper asked, "What exactly is the difference?"

"About the same as between you dating *your* boss and you dating his next-door neighbor."

"Pul—leeze." Like that was a good example.

"The only neighbor I've met is an eleven-year-old boy, and my boss doesn't even…"

"Doesn't even what?"

Notice I'm here. That's what Piper was going to say, anyway. Only he had noticed tonight. Absently, she ran a knuckle down her cheek as she remembered his kind gesture.

"Piper?"

"Sorry," she said, shaking off the memory. "I lost track of what I was about to say. And *you* still haven't answered my question. Are you dating Stuart Duchenko?"

There was a definite darkening to her sister's blush. "For now, yes."

A different kind of heaviness took up space in Piper's stomach. The same uncomfortable feeling she used to get as a kid when waiting to be picked for dodgeball. She was always left for last.

Ignoring the sensation, she pushed her lips into a smile. "No way! That's great! I'm so happy for you." She was, childish reaction aside. She had no reason to feel anything *but* happy, really. It was just her pity party making its reappearance.

"Don't go making a big deal," her sister was saying. "The two of us are having fun together, that's all. It's nothing serious."

The sparkle in Patience's eyes said otherwise, but Piper kept the thought to herself. Patience would admit the truth soon enough.

The two of them talked and joked while Piper worked and for a little while, her loneliness receded.

"Why aren't you making some fancy French dish?" Patience asked as she was putting the casserole in the oven.

"Because I felt like macaroni and cheese. Would you feel better if I called it *macaroni au fromage*?"

"A little." From her chair on the other side of the world, her sister frowned again. "Are you sure you're all right? You mentioned your boss earlier. Is he still treating you okay?"

Once again, a paper towel and a smile flashed before Piper's eyes. "He's treating me fine."

"That sounded weird."

"What do you mean?"

"The way you said 'fine' with a long sigh."

Piper rolled her eyes. As if her sigh could be any longer or dreamier-sounding than the ones her sister made. "How should I say it? He treats me fine. We hardly see each other." Today's encounters notwithstanding. "Not everyone socializes with their boss, you know. I meant Ana," she added quickly before Patience got the wrong idea.

"So long as he isn't giving you a hard time."

"I swear, he isn't."

They talked a little longer, mostly about silly stuff. Patience told a few stories about Nigel the cat and about how things were going with Stuart. Piper lied about how well school was going. By the time they said goodbye, she'd cooked and eaten her casserole. She would have said that the night was exactly what she needed, except that as soon as she turned off the computer, her melancholy returned stronger than ever.

"It's Hollywood's fault," she said to the Eiffel Tower a little while later. "All those movies making Paris look so wonderful. Leading a woman to hope life might be more magical under French skies."

There was a smudge on the glass. Breathing some fog on the pane, she wiped at it with her sleeve. Patience would be horrified by her casualness. Her sister took cleaning very seriously.

Maybe if she tried a little harder. Gave more effort in class, learned to appreciate her surroundings more. Maybe then she could work up the enthusiasm she was supposed to feel for this adventure. Right now, she only felt tired. The carbohydrates were kicking in. Merging with her sad mood and killing what was left of her cleaning ambitions.

Discarding her plans to dig out the cleaning supplies, she sank into a nearby chair. The same one she found Frederic sleeping in this morning, she realized. Outside, the tower twinkled mockingly. Leaning her head back, she watched the lights dance. They were beautiful, weren't they?

"Easy chair to fall asleep in, no?"

The voice close to her ear was deep and rough. Piper jumped to her feet. Grabbing the first thing she could find, she whirled around ready to attack.

Frederic raised his hands in mock surrender. "I'm sorry. I didn't mean to scare you."

"You didn't..." Considering she was wielding a pillow as a weapon, she gave up the argument. "I wasn't expecting you home so early, is all." It was early, right? *Please say it was early.*

"My date wasn't feeling well, so we left the concert at intermission." His eyes narrowed, as if zooming in on her. Too late, Piper realized she still wore her chef's jacket instead of her uniform. "You were working hard?"

"No. I mean, I planned to but I..."

"I am joking."

"Oh." Thank goodness the lights were dim and he couldn't see how red her cheeks were.

"If I recall, I suggested you take the night off to relax. I'm glad you did." He crossed to the window. Hands clasped behind his back, he stood looking out at the tower.

One of the things Piper had noticed while working for Frederic was the way he concentrated so intently on whatever he was doing. Walking. Looking out the window. Some of the focus she attributed to his bad eyes, but lousy vision didn't explain the power behind his movements. He moved with such deliberation. As though nothing could deter him from the action at hand. The guy could give Chef Despelteau a run for his money when it came to laser glares, that's for sure. She could only imagine what it was like to be one of his students.

Or one of his dates, for that matter.

All of a sudden she realized those slate-colored eyes were looking at her. He'd said something, and she missed it. Again, she thanked the dim

lighting for protecting her from bigger embarrassment. "I'm sorry, what did you say?"

"I asked if you were enjoying your year in Paris
so far."

You mean her crying jag earlier didn't give him
a clue? "It's a beautiful city."

"That it is. Have you done much sightseeing?"

"A little." When she first arrived and was still
in her starry-eyed phase. After a couple weeks,
however, solo sightseeing lost its luster. "Between
class and work, I haven't had much time."

"That is too bad. You should make sure you
see as much as possible. You never know when
you'll have another chance."

"I'll try to remember that." For some reason,
Piper felt as though he was talking about more
than sightseeing. Or maybe fatigue was making
her read too deeply between the lines. For all she
knew, this was his normal way of making conversation. He approached everything else with
intensity; why wouldn't he approach talking the
same way?

Regardless of the reason, the exchange left a hum in the air that made her antsy. Piper couldn't help thinking how crisp and elegant he looked in his summer suit. Meanwhile, she was growing more aware of her wrinkled jacket by the second. Not to mention the smell of onion and cheddar cheese clinging to her fingers.

Suddenly, she needed some space. Setting down her pillow, she announced, "I'm going to finish cleaning the kitchen." The kitchen was spotless, but she needed some kind of excuse. Then, whether because of the thickened atmosphere or something else, she added, "I'm really sorry, too, about my meltdown earlier."

"Already forgotten, Piper. I hope whatever caused your distress is gone by tomorrow."

"I hope so, too." Not very likely, but a girl could hope. She went to say good-night, but Frederic had already turned his back to the room, his attention once again on the scene outside his window.

Must have been a trick of the shadows. Standing there with his hands behind his back, he suddenly looked alone and far away. *Maybe I'm not the only lonely person in Paris.* The thought was in her head before Piper could stop it.

Frederic Lafontaine, lonely. Sure. Now she knew she was tired.

CHAPTER TWO

THE NEXT MORNING, Piper called Marie Rougeau-Montpelier and introduced herself. To her surprise, the elderly woman said she would be thrilled to meet with her, especially once Piper mentioned her brother's artwork. She invited Piper to visit after lunch. The appointment meant skipping a day of class, but Piper didn't really mind. A day off, in fact, might do her some good. Help her get her head back into the game.

Marie's address, which turned out to be a luxury tower near La Défense, the business district just outside the city, was easier to find than she expected. Not wanting to ring the woman's bell before she was expected, Piper found herself wandering around La Grande Arche, the city's twentieth-century version of the Arc de Triomphe. It was the perfect summer's day. Not too hot, not too cold. Being lunchtime, the square was filled with people. Business executives sat on nearby steps soaking up the sun while tourists and others lounged on the grass in the nearby park. Piper strolled the perimeter and watched as they laughed and chatted with each other. Was this what Frederic meant when he told her to see as much of the city as possible?

Thinking of her boss made her insides sag. He was nowhere to be found when she woke up this morning. That didn't surprise her, he was nowhere to be found most of the time, but Piper sort of hoped that after last night, the routine might have changed. She still couldn't shake the image of him staring out his salon window. Looking so solitary and distant. So *alone*.

There's a word for what you're doing, you know. Projecting or connecting, something like that. Whatever the word, she needed to stop. Just because she was in another sad mood didn't mean her boss was too.

Her feet hurt, protesting having to wear sandals after months of wearing sturdy shoes. She looked around for a café where she could give them a break. There was one on the corner with a maroon-and-white awning that wasn't overly crowded. Helping herself to one of the empty rattan chairs that lined the sidewalk, she had just pulled out her cell phone when she heard a familiar-sounding voice ordering an espresso.

No way. She looked to her left. Even with aviator sunglasses covering his face, she recognized Frederic's profile instantly.

He was alone. At least the chair across from him was empty, and judging from the way his long legs were stretched out to claim the table's real estate, he wasn't expecting a guest to arrive anytime soon. Piper's eyes traveled their length, from his wingtips to the muscular thighs that disappeared beneath the tablecloth. In contrast to last night, today he looked the picture of ease.

Must be nice to feel so confident instead of having to fake it all the time. And to be that good-looking. Patience was always saying that being beautiful wasn't all it was cracked up to be. Piper wouldn't know. She was never someone people thought of as beautiful. When the guys in high school made fun of Patience's job, they did so with a glaze of lust in their eyes. No one's eyes ever glazed for Piper.

Just then, as though sensing her stare, Frederic turned in her direction. Piper started to shrink back into the shadows, then caught herself and waved instead. He didn't wave back.

She was about to take offense when she realized she wasn't in his field of vision. Smoothing her skirt, she walked toward his table.

"Bonjour, monsieur," she greeted with a smile.

The sound of an American accent jarred Frederic from his thoughts. He knew of only one person who spoke French with an accent like that. Blinking out of his fog, he found a whirl of yellow and red in his line of sight. Lifting his eyes, he saw a familiar brunette head. "Piper? Where did you come from?"

"Two tables over. I waved, but you weren't paying attention."

She was being polite. They both knew he didn't wave because she wasn't sitting in his field of view.

"Lost in thought," he replied, continuing the pretense.

"I'm not bothering you, am I?" Piper's question brought him back.

"Not at all. I'm killing time after an appointment is all." Yet another pointless meeting with his ophthalmologist. He went every few months simply to hear that his eyes were still diseased.

"And you?"

"Killing time before an appointment, actually."

Sitting back in his chair, Frederic found himself wishing he'd been paying attention when she approached. Whenever he saw Piper at the apartment, she wore either her chef's jacket or that awful maid uniform that was the antithesis of every French maid fantasy ever written. This sundress, however… The bright colors definitely suited her better. Plus, there was an expanse of flesh around her shoulders he didn't normally get to enjoy.

"Are you meeting a classmate?" he asked. A date would certainly explain the dress. Why he was suddenly intrigued by her social life, Frederic wasn't sure, except that the memory of her crying by the kitchen counter refused to leave him. He found it odd, an attractive American—and she was attractive as that expanse of skin attested—spending her evenings in Paris alone.

"I'm supposed to meet with someone at the Rose d'Arms," she said. "It's a retirement home a block or so from here."

"Looking for a surrogate grandmother?"

"Hardly," she said with a laugh. A very pleasant-sounding laugh, too. Like bells. "I'm doing a favor for my sister."

"At a retirement home?"

"It's a long story. I won't bore you with the details. I really just stopped by to say hello. I'll let you get back to whatever it was you were…"

"Please. Stay. We can kill time together."

"Are you sure?"

There was hesitancy in her voice. Frederic couldn't blame her. Eight months of hardly talking, and now here they were on their third conversation in two days. "I wouldn't have offered if I wasn't sure," he told her. "There is no reason for the two of us to sit at separate tables when we are both by ourselves. Besides, you have me intrigued."

The café had arranged the tables as so many cafés in the city did, with the seats side by side so that patrons could enjoy the view. As Piper slipped into the seat beside his, Frederic was struck by an aroma of vanilla and spices that made his mouth water. "Did you bake today?" he asked.

"No. I skipped class. Why?"

"No reason." Who knew a person could smell delicious? "Tell me this long story of yours."

Piper took a deep breath. "Apparently, Ana, my sister's boss, lived with an artist here in Paris in the seventies and posed for a bunch of paintings. Her great-nephew, Stuart, is hoping to surprise her with one as a gift, so Patience asked me if I would talk to the artist's sister to see if any of his paintings survived."

"Doesn't your sister realize there are easier ways to track down an artist's work? If he is well-known…"

"This is where it gets complicated."

She paused while the waitress brought his espresso and she placed her order.

"Complicated how?"

"The artist died in an accident a long time ago. According to Ana, he would have been huge— like Picasso huge—but then Theodore Duchenko went and bought up…"

"Wait…" Frederic needed to go back a step. "Did you say Theodore *Duchenko*?"

Piper nodded. "That's right. Patience works for his sister, Ana Duchenko."

Unbelievable. Duchenko Silver was world re-nowned. Frederic knew curators who gushed over adding a piece of the famed Russian silver to their collections. As for the late Theodore Duchenko, the man had been considered one of the most ruthless tycoons of the twentieth century. "You're saying that you're trying to track down a portrait of Ana Duchenko."

"Not just a portrait. A nude," Piper replied. "Nigel painted a bunch, and they were supposedly pretty racy, which is why…"

"Duchenko wanted them destroyed," he finished for her. "This is astounding. The Duchenko name, it is…well, let us say that if a portrait still exists, the significance in terms of pop culture alone would be immeasurable."

"I don't think Stuart cares if the painting has any kind of value—he just wants to give his aunt back a piece of her history. The way my sister tells it, Ana truly loved the man."

The waitress returned with her café au lait. "It's all very tragic, really," Piper said, taking a sip.

Tragic but exciting. Frederic found his curiosity piqued in a way he hadn't felt in years. Not since his university days. "There is nothing like the thrill of discovering a new artist," he told her. "The euphoria, it hits you like a…" The sexual metaphor was too crude to share with a woman. He settled for saying "There are few pleasures like it. I envy you."

"The whole thing is probably a long shot."

"Perhaps," he said, reaching for his drink. It quite probably was, in fact. "But long shot or not, the chase is always exciting."

"Want to come with me?"

Frederic set his cup down with a *clink* so he could focus his gaze on her. "Pardon?"

"You just said you envied my going on the hunt. Besides, I don't know anything about art. What if there's a giant painting of Ana hanging on this woman's wall? How will I know if it's worth Stuart's money?"

And she thought *he* was the best person to evaluate? "You just said the painting wasn't about value."

"It isn't." There was silence as she shifted in her chair. When she spoke again, Frederic heard a change in her voice. It became lower, with less spark. "Never mind. It was only a suggestion."

"No, I'd love to join you." Unsettled by the sadness he thought he heard in her voice, he spoke without thinking.

The smile worked its way back into her voice. "Awesome! I'll finish my coffee and we'll go."

A visit to a retirement home, Frederic said to himself as he sipped his espresso. *To meet with an old woman. No harm in that.*

Why, then, did he feel as if he was getting involved in something more?

There wasn't, of course, an undiscovered painting hanging in Marie's apartment. Only a very tall, pinched-looking woman wearing a velvet tracksuit. She greeted the two of them with a wide smile. "A professor. How exciting," she gushed, squeezing his hand. "Please come in."

"I knew you'd be a hit," Piper murmured as she stepped inside.

Frederic grinned in response. His insides were feeling the thrill of the hunt.

While he still wasn't entirely sure why Piper had asked him to come along, he'd decided to embrace the opportunity. Who knew when another chance would cross his path? Or, for that matter, come with such an attractive package. Piper was far enough into the room that he could finally see her figure. She had curves a sculpture would love. Soft and supple. The kind meant to be traced by a person's hands.

That's it. He was getting rid of the maid's uniform.

"What period do you study, Professor?" Marie was asking. The older woman was already limping across the sitting room en route to the bookcase.

"Medieval. Pre-Romanesque mostly."

"Nigel would have called you stuck in the past, but then he prided himself on being antiestablishment. We all did back then. Please, have a seat."

She gestured to a sofa barely large enough to deserve the label. Feeling overly large, he perched on the edge of the seat and wondered how a woman Marie's height could ever sit comfortably. The cushion dipped and Piper sat beside him. Vanilla and spice teased his nostrils again. It was like walking into the most pleasant bakery on earth every time the woman sat down.

"He had such promise, my brother. My mother used to brag he knew how to paint before he could walk. An exaggeration, I'm sure. Come to think of it, though, I can't remember a time when he wasn't drawing or painting or something."

Reaching up, she pulled out what looked like a large plastic binder and opened it up. "This is him here," she said. "Five years old and he'd already won his first competition."

She set the album on Frederic's lap. The old

photo was too small and blurry for him to focus much on, but he leaned forward and pretended all the same. Piper leaned in as well, her left knee knocking against his as she shifted angles. Frederic sucked in his breath at the awareness shooting up his thigh. Even with two layers of material, he felt every bump and bone pressed against him.

"Impressive," he murmured. Although he wasn't sure if he meant Nigel's childhood art or Piper's knee.

"He could have done so much," Marie said. "We all told him to stop riding that motorbike, but he was stubborn." A crack worked its way into the end of her voice. "I'm sorry," she said, pressing a fist to her lips. "It's been a long time since I've talked about Nigel at all."

"We're sorry if we're bringing up bad memories," Piper remarked.

"That's all right. They aren't all bad. In some ways, I think Nigel wanted to die young. He once told me that art only reached the masses once you were gone."

"I could name a few living painters who might disagree," Frederic replied.

Her resulting smile was watery, but strong. "I never said his theory made sense. In the end, it didn't matter anyway, because his work never reached anyone."

Because Theodore Duchenko ordered it destroyed.

"That is why we're here," Piper said. "My sister works for Ana Duchenko."

Every ounce of humor disappeared from Marie's face. "That family destroyed my brother," she said, stiffening. "I was only a child, but I remember how my parents cursed Theodore Duchenko and the rest of them."

To her credit, Piper didn't stiffen in return. He always thought how a person reacted when challenged said a lot about them. His housekeeper, it appeared, knew how to stand tall. "From what

I hear, Theodore Duchenko deserved cursing," she said. "What he did was awful."

"It was an outrage. Ruining my brother's life, decimating his art all because he was afraid his family would be embarrassed." The rest of her rant disappeared in a soft mutter.

"For what it's worth, Ana never spoke to her brother again because of what he did."

Marie stopped muttering. "She didn't?"

"No. My sister says Ana blames her brother for Nigel's death as much as you do. She never married, either."

"Because of Nigel?"

"She loved your brother very much."

This was the part of the story that made Frederic uncomfortable. Love stealing a young heiress's future. The idea of a life stolen out from under you struck a little too close to home.

Marie was back at the bookcase, a long purple silhouette whose head was cut off in darkness. "I only met her once," she was saying. "Nigel brought her to Sunday dinner and told us all she was his muse. My parents were not happy. I remember my father whispering that Ana 'looked expensive.'" Frederic could picture the scene. Nigel, their starving artist son, walking in with his wealthy seventeen-year-old lover.

"I know that Theodore tried to destroy all of Nigel's paintings." Piper's knee brushed Frederic's again as she shifted in her seat. His entire leg felt the contact this time. "We're hoping, though, he might have missed one or two."

"If one existed, don't you think my family would have kept it?"

"Perhaps there was a sale he made before Theodore arrived in France," Frederic suggested. "Or a gift he gave to a friend."

Marie shook her head. "I have no idea. The only paintings left of Nigel's that we have are a couple small landscapes he did for my mother while he was in art school."

"It's all right," Piper replied. "We figured it was a long shot."

Perhaps, thought Frederic, but she had clearly hoped. Her disappointment was palpable.

Whenever one of his students felt let down, he made a point of reminding them life was full of disappointments.

Right now with Piper, all he wanted was to squeeze her hand. Reassure rather than remind. It was definitely not like him.

Marie was still talking. "To be honest, even if a portrait of Ana did survive, I'm not sure my parents would have kept it. They didn't want anything to do with the Duchenkos."

"No," Piper said. "I don't suppose they would."

"My brother did have a friend who might know. He owned an art gallery in the Marais. A very successful one, I believe. His name was Gaspard."

Frederic looked up. "You don't mean Gaspard Theroux?"

"Yes, that's him."

"You know him?" Piper asked.

"Galerie Gaspard Theroux is one of the most respected galleries in Paris."

"Gaspard and Nigel were very close. If he is still alive, he might know whether any of Nigel's early Ana studies sold."

"I'll tell you one thing," Frederic said as they were walking across the square a short while later. "If Gaspard represented Nigel's work, he must have been very talented. The gallery is known for discovering the best rising talent in Europe. I've bought a couple pieces from Gaspard's son, Bernard. He doesn't have quite the same eye as his father, but he does well."

Piper didn't care how good an eye the guy had. All she cared about was that her search hadn't reached a dead end. It took her by surprise just how disappointed she was when Marie first said the paintings were gone. The repeated stories of Ana and Nigel's love affair had gotten to her.

She turned so she could get a better view of the man walking beside her. Inviting Frederic to join her was a total impulse. He sounded so animated when he was talking about Nigel's work being a significant discovery. Plus, she liked the idea of his company in case Marie wasn't as friendly as she had sounded on the phone. There wasn't a woman of any age who wouldn't like seeing a man who looked like Frederic on her doorstep.

Now as it turned out, he turned out to be an invaluable resource. "I don't suppose you know if Gaspard Theroux is still alive, do you?"

"He is, but he has had health problems the past few years. His mind…" Frederic gestured with his hands as to say he didn't know.

That's what Piper was afraid of. She combed her fingers through her hair with a sigh. At least she had a place to start. "Maybe his son knows something. What did you say his name was?"

"Bernard."

"I'll give him a call tomorrow." Maybe his father kept records from those days.

"Good luck. Bernard is not the easiest person to reach. He tends to ignore people who aren't serious collectors. Even his gallery is open by appointment only."

Great. How was she going to get an appointment? Make a pest of herself until he called back?

Or... An idea struck her. "He returns your phone calls, doesn't he?"

"Of course. We've done business for years. Are you asking me to call Bernard for you?"

"Would you? It might make him more willing to talk with me. Then, if the painting gets discovered, you can take partial credit."

Frederic laughed.

"What?" Piper had heard him laugh before, but never with such a teasing tone. In spite of his sunglasses, the smile lit up his face. She liked how he threw his head back, too, as if tossing the laugh toward the sky. "You don't want credit?"

"On the contrary, recognition is always welcome."

"Then what's so funny?"

"Nothing."

Something amused him. Was it her? If so, why

didn't she feel a knot in her stomach, the way she usually did when people laughed at her? Instead, she had a warm squishy feeling running all through her.

"Will you call Bernard?"

"Yes, I will. As soon as I get back to the university."

"Thank you! You're awesome." She was so glad she asked him along today. Finally a good day in Paris. She threw her arms around his neck and hugged him.

It didn't dawn on her what she had done until she felt the corner of his belt buckle against her rib cage. With heat shooting to her toes, she released her grip, and prayed her face wasn't as flushed as it felt.

"Um…thank you," she stammered.

"My pleasure," he replied. Piper thought she saw a hint of a smile as he spoke, but double-checking meant looking into his face. Considering her skin was on fire, staring at the cell phone he was now dialing seemed a safer bet. "As enjoyable as this afternoon has been," she heard him say, "I have a faculty meeting I need to attend. Should I have Michel drop you off at the house?"

Meaning sit with him in the backseat of his car? "That's all right, I'll take the Métro." Another safe bet. "I want to stop at the farmers' market, anyway."

"Suit yourself. I'll let you know what Bernard says."

Piper watched as he headed to the same café where their afternoon started, moving with his usual careful, deliberate grace. Clearly, her hug affected only one of them. But then, did she really expect otherwise?

CHAPTER THREE

WHEN SHE RETURNED from class the following day, Frederic was waiting in the main salon. "We've got a meeting with Bernard in half an hour," he said. "The car is on the way."

"We?" she repeated, making sure she heard correctly. This was the first they'd spoken since she rushed off last night, and considering her overreaction to his hug, there was a good chance she misheard. "You're coming?"

"I have to. I'm invested in the search now. Plus, Bernard has a painting he thinks I might be interested in."

"Oh." So she hadn't heard wrong. Her stomach gave a tiny bounce at the discovery. "I'll go get ready."

She rushed through the kitchen, unbuttoning

her jacket as she went. Frederic worked fast. Sure, he said he would call yesterday, but she fully expected to be dropped in priority when he got to his meeting. *He did say he was invested*, she reminded herself. Still, the idea that her errand stayed atop his to-do list left her strangely flattered.

Yesterday's yellow dress was on the back of her chair. Her one good summer outfit. She'd foolishly assumed she'd be shopping in Paris.

Better than jeans and a T-shirt, she reminded herself while slipping the dress over her head. The skirt was wrinkled from yesterday, but serviceable. Only Frederic would know she was wearing the same outfit. Assuming he even paid attention to what she wore. Grabbing her sandals, she hurried back to the salon.

"That was fast," Frederic remarked when he saw her. He, she noticed, looked as crisp and perfect as ever in his linen blazer.

"You said to hurry."

"I'm not used to people understanding what

that means. You forget, I spend my day with university students. They have a different view of time."

He opened the front door and gestured for her to step outside. "Shall we?"

Like many of Paris's art galleries, the Galerie Gaspard Theroux was in the Marais, the historic district, near the Place des Vosges. Piper stepped into the sunshine with a silent sigh of relief.

"I have to admit," Piper said as she stepped out of the cab, "I like this section of the city much better." The business district was beautiful but modern. But here… This was the Paris she dreamed about. "The statues in the middle of the street and the cobblestones…it's all so…"

"Romantic?"

His drily spoken answer made her blush. "I know, typical American, right?"

"Yes, but also no. This is my favorite part of the city, too. As impressive as skyscrapers are, you cannot top classic French design. Did you know this square is one of the first examples of urban planning? Henri IV was ahead of his time." He swept his arm wide in an animated arc. "It was also one of the few times all the building fronts were designed the same way. See the arcades lining the perimeter?"

He went on, talking about the different sections of the building, architectural and historical details Piper wished she could appreciate. She was far more entertained by the expression on his face. His enthusiasm was obvious, despite the sunglasses masking his eyes. The way he spoke was reverent. So much lighter than his usual tone, which was so serious it bordered on short, she could have listened to him go on forever. Good thing Chef Despelteau didn't have such a voice. She'd be so distracted by the way the words dripped off his tongue she'd never get any recipe right.

"For an art history expert, you sure know a lot about architecture," she teased.

There was no mistaking the pink spots peering out beneath the rims of his aviators. "In my opinion, architecture is its own form of art," he told her. "The gargoyles of Notre Dame, for example. Or Louis the thirteenth's statue in the park. I appreciate the effort that goes into creating beauty. When I think of this section of the city, especially, and the disasters and wars it has survived, I cannot help but be impressed.

"Come," he said, taking her elbow, "Bernard's gallery is on the western side." Taking her by the elbow, he led her toward the shaded walkway on the far end of the plaza.

Art galleries and antiques stores lined the sidewalk beneath the arch. As they walked, Piper tried to appreciate the various pieces in the windows, but she was too distracted by the lingering sensation on her elbow. Twice she needed to check, even though Frederic released her seconds after touching her.

"Bernard's gallery is number thirty-three," Frederic said. "He often keeps the door locked. We might have to ring the bell."

"A locked store and visits by appointment. You're right, he is selective about his customers."

"He can afford to be."

"Must be nice. Hopefully I make the cut."

"You will," Frederic said with a smile. "You are with me."

Piper spotted the gallery before he did. A quick tug showed the door to be unlocked. As Frederic opened it wide, a bell tinkled overhead.

"Bonjour!" Bernard Theroux appeared from the back of the gallery. He was a tall, slender man with a wispy gray mustache and thinning gray hair that he wore combed back. The moment he saw Frederic, his porcelain features broke into a grin and he began speaking in rapid French, far too fast for Piper to keep up.

"I'm sorry," he said, switching to perfect English. "I was lecturing someone about being a stranger."

"And I was explaining how busy work has been."

"I can vouch for that," Piper remarked. "He's

hardly ever home." The comment made her sound like a disgruntled wife. "I mean, he works a lot." That didn't sound much better.

Thankfully, the gallery owner was more interested in dragging Frederic toward one of the paintings. "Like I told you on the phone, you are going to love this piece. He's a new artist out of Prague—I discovered him on my last trip. Wait until you see what he does with shadow."

"I'm sure it's spectacular," Frederic said. "But before I look at anything, Piper had some questions she wanted to ask. About a friend of your father's."

Although his sigh said he'd rather talk about the painter from Prague, Bernard turned to Piper. "Of course. Although like I told Frederic, my father had a lot of painter friends over the years. If it was before I was born, I doubt I can help you."

"He wasn't only a friend—he was possibly a client," Piper replied. "His sister thinks your father sold one or two of his paintings."

She reached into her purse for her cell phone.

Patience had emailed her a snapshot that featured one of the paintings. "I'm hoping that a record of the sale still exists. The artist's name was Nigel Rougeau. The painting would have looked like this one."

She held out her phone so he could see the image. Instantly, Bernard's eyes became saucers.

"Dear God, I don't believe it. This is the painting you're looking for? This nude?"

"Yes?" Although she suddenly wasn't sure she should say so. The gleam in Bernard's eyes made her nervous. "Why?"

"I grew up looking at that woman."

"You—you did?"

"Yes, she hung in our dining room."

No way. Piper couldn't believe her good luck. She'd been prepared to strike out, and here the man was saying he'd seen the painting. "Does your father still have the painting?"

Bernard shook his head. "I'm afraid not. I sold most of the collection when we closed down his house. To pay his expenses. The nude was sold with the others."

She should have known the search wouldn't end easily. Still, there was hope. "You wouldn't know the name of the man who bought it, would you?" she asked.

"I keep records for every painting," Bernard replied with a sniff.

"Could we get the name?" Frederic asked. Piper started. She had assumed he was studying the painting, and so his deep voice caught her off guard.

"Yes, but it will take me a few minutes to pull up the record on the computer."

"Thank you," Piper said, speaking as much to Frederic as to Bernard. "I truly appreciate the help."

"I'll be back with the information as soon as I can. In the meantime, you now have plenty of time to study the Biskup. It's called *Zoufalstvi*." His smile was smug as he gestured toward the painting. "I know you're going to be as impressed with his style as I am."

Piper walked up to the painting. It was contemporary art, a mash-up of black, white and red, which she assumed had some kind of meaning. She understood the price well enough. She paid less for the entire year of culinary school.

"What do you think?" she asked, looking over her shoulder.

Frederic stood where she left him, taking in the painting from a distance. "Interesting," was all he said.

"Your friend isn't really expecting you to buy it today, is he?"

"Oh, he is. Bernard never jokes when it comes to artwork. If he says the painting is a good investment, then I'm sure it is."

"And you would what? Just write a check if you liked it?"

"If I liked it."

She shook her head. The idea of writing a check for an amount that took her months upon months to save—and that was with pinching every single penny—boggled her mind. Here Frederic talked about dropping that amount like he was buying a new shirt. "Do you like it?" she had to ask.

"Do you?" he asked back.

"Honest opinion?" He nodded. "I'm not sure what I'm looking at. It all looks like a bunch of colors to me."

She squinted, trying to make sense of the image. In a way, it was similar to the other paintings in Frederic's house. They too were modern, but warmer and with brighter colors. This painting was definitely not warm. It did conjure up emotion, a weirdly familiar feeling in the pit of her stomach, but she wouldn't call the sensation pleasant. Nor would she want to feel it every day.

"It's a very sad-looking painting," she said.

"I should hope so." Footsteps sounded on the wood floor, and suddenly Frederic was at her elbow. "*Zoufalstvi* is Czech for *desperation*."

No wonder it left her feeling empty. "I don't see

why anyone would want to buy such a depressing picture. But then, I'm not much of an artist."

"Really? I thought chefs considered cooking an art form."

"Great cooking, sure. All the best chefs are artists." As Chef Despelteau reminded them so often. "But I was talking about *art* art. You know, paintings and stuff." She turned her attention to a different piece. "Growing up, the fanciest thing on our walls was a framed poster of Monet's *Water Lilies*. I'm going to go out on a limb and say Bernard doesn't sell posters."

"No, he does not."

"Too bad." They stood quietly in front of the painting. This second one had prettier colors, but the image wasn't nearly as powerful to look at.

That was it, Piper realized suddenly. Why the Biskup painting seemed so familiar. The image reminded her of Frederic. He, too, was forceful and compelling. Where did the sadness come in, though? Her boss could hardly be described as sad.

He was solitary, though. For all his activity, the man was alone much of the time. If there were family and friends in his life, they certainly didn't visit the house.

"I hope you don't buy the painting," she said aloud.

He turned at that moment and looked into her face, his eyes grayer than usual. "Why not?"

"Because I—" What was she supposed to say? Because it made her think sad thoughts about him? Like she told herself yesterday, she was pushing her thoughts onto him. Solitary didn't mean lonely. For all she knew, Frederic was simply a man who liked his privacy.

Her answer didn't matter anyway, because the moment she met his eyes, any explanation she might have come up with disappeared. All this time, she'd thought his eyes were gray, but they were really far softer. Like feathers or a fluffy cloud of smoke. She could almost feel the haze in the air, surrounding her like a warm plume.

A shock of hair had fallen over one eyebrow,

knocked loose when he took his sunglasses off. The dark strands begged to be brushed aside.

"Piper?" she heard him ask.

Oh, good Lord, she was staring at him with her jaw half open like an idiot.

"What I meant," she said, tucking imaginary hair behind her ear, "was that I don't like the idea you might have to buy something on my account."

"You're afraid I won't know how to say no?"

"Of—of course you can. Say no, that is. I just don't want…"

"Don't worry," he said, saving her from making a bigger fool of herself than she already had. "I stopped acquiring pieces a while ago. Bernard forgets I no longer have the eye for detail I once had."

Piper's heart gave a little twist at the wistful shadow that flickered over his features. Bernard wasn't the only one who'd forgotten. The man was so capable and self-assured. *Who wouldn't forget?*

"I'll take that as a compliment," Frederic said with a chuckle.

Meaning she'd spoken her thoughts aloud. The floor could swallow her up any time now.

"So, what do you think? Do you not love the expressive way he plays light on shadow?" Bernard came around the corner, saving her. "I am predicting this artist will be very popular. Already, several serious collectors have put him on their watch lists. This would be your chance to acquire a piece before his popularity drives the price up."

"Don't you mean while you still have him on a string?" Frederic replied. The teasing retort caught Piper by surprise. "Bernard only pushes this hard when he's personally involved," he explained to her. "Isn't that right, Bernard?"

The gallery owner's cheeks turned crimson. "I do predict big things for him. You know I only push if they have talent."

"Yes, I know. Did you find the address?"

"I did." He turned to Piper. "The painting is

called *Ana Reclining*. I'm ashamed that I didn't remember. It was purchased by a man named John Allen. Whether or not he still owns the piece, I do not know."

Piper took the slip of paper. This was fantastic. They had a real live name. Wait until she told Patience. "Gloucestershire," she read. "England?"

"Northwest of London," Frederic replied.

There was no way of knowing if the address and phone were current, either. Still, it was a start. A very good start.

"Two days ago, we didn't know if a painting even existed," she remarked when she and Frederic stepped outside. "And now here I am with a name. I feel like Piper Rush, art detective."

"It's always exciting when a lost work is discovered. Did you know they once discovered a seventeenth-century Le Brun hanging in a suite at the Ritz-Carlton?"

"I wouldn't put this painting on the same level. But Ana's nephew will be excited." She had no idea who Le Brun was, but seventeenth-century sounded important. "Lucky for him that Bernard's father decided to keep one of the paintings for himself."

"Indeed." Although they were standing in the shade, he lowered his sunglasses in place anyway. As the dark lenses slid over his features, Piper felt a flutter in her stomach. Relief that she'd been saved from whatever that strange sensation was when she looked into his eyes before. As it was, the moment had left her with this restless, jumbly sensation, as if her insides drank too much caffeine.

"So what is your next move, Madame Detective?" he asked her.

"Give the information to Patience so they can track John Allen down, I suppose."

"You don't sound very excited about the prospect."

In a strange way, she wasn't. "I'll miss playing detective," she said. "The past couple days have been a nice break in my routine." That included the unexpected time she spent with him. Having finished her favor for Patience, life would go back to normal. Normal and lonely.

"You don't have to stop."

She laughed. "You know another piece of art that needs to be tracked down?"

"No, but the search for this one is not complete."

True. Bernard's information could be woefully out of date. "Guess I should make a phone call or two to make sure my lead pans out." She added the detective lingo on purpose, just because it was fun to use.

"And if need be, travel to England to inspect the canvas."

"Now that might be going a little too far." Piper could see herself now, knocking on John Allen's door and asking if she could inspect his nude portrait.

"Why? Do you not want a chance to see the painting up close?"

"Sure, but… Would you?"

"For a chance to discover a lost painting, I'd go anywhere. I've traveled farther for far less."

"Well, if you don't mind, I'll start with a few phone calls," Piper replied.

Just then, the car arrived, pulling to the curb with the soft *beep* of the horn. "Sorry to keep you waiting," Michel said as he hurried to open the passenger door.

The switch from bright sunlight to the car's interior temporary plunged Piper into darkness, making her blink several times before she could properly see her surroundings. Today was the first time she'd ever ridden in a limousine, and while she told herself the experience was no different from riding in a cab, it was. For one thing, cabs didn't have supple seats that molded to your body. And they definitely didn't smell like leather and spicy aftershave. Yesterday's decision to ride the Métro had definitely been the right one. In fact, she inhaled deeply, she wondered if she shouldn't have made the same decision this afternoon.

The car itself was not nearly as fancy as she expected. On TV, the limousines always had skylights and crystal decanters. Frederic went for a sleek simplicity. All the more impressive, really. Reminded her of how quality food didn't need a lot of trimmings to taste impressive. Frederic didn't need trimmings, either.

If only she didn't feel so jittery. She'd love to blame the feeling on being out of her element, but that wouldn't explain why the sensation didn't fully grip her until she lost herself in Frederic's gray eyes. Or why the quiet determination in his voice just now turned her insides upside down.

Frederic slipped into the seat beside her and the driver shut the door, sealing them together in the dimness. If only he weren't so tall and broad-shouldered. A smaller man would take up less space. His body heat wouldn't cross the distance to buffet her body. It turned the air thick.

Piper smoothed her skirt. The yellow was suddenly way too bright for the space. "Thank you again for arranging the meeting with Bernard," she said.

"You already thanked me twice on the trip here. There's no need to do it again."

"I'm excited the trip was successful, is all." Not to mention talking eased her tension and thank you was the only thing she could think of. "I feel like I owe you something. After all, you did give up part of your afternoon to help me. You could have let me deal with Bernard on my own."

He laughed, teeth white in the shadows. "If I had, you would still be leaving messages on his machine."

True enough. Bernard was a character. "We have a name for guys like him back home."

"There are names for guys like him everywhere," Frederic replied. "And again, I was glad to help. I'm as intrigued by this painting as you are. It's been a while since I've played art detective myself. If this painting is as good as Bernard believes, it will be quite the discovery."

Piper thought of his comment from earlier,

about traveling farther for less. "Do you miss it? Tracking down art?"

"Yes, but what can you do?" He shrugged. "Life is what it is. It's not as though I can change anything, is it?"

"I guess not." Remembering his wistful expression at the gallery, Piper couldn't help wondering if he was as Zen about his circumstances as he sounded. If she were losing her sight, she would be railing against the universe. She certainly wouldn't talk about it as matter-of-factly as he did.

She turned to steal a look at him, only to find he was looking back at her with that unnaturally intense gaze of his.

"I'm glad helping me didn't keep you from anything important," she said, jumping back to the original conversation. Her attention returned to her lap and the imaginary wrinkles she needed to smooth away.

Leather crinkled as Frederic shifted, too.

"Definitely not," he replied. "The only thing

on my schedule is tonight's meeting of the Société pour la Conservation Artistique. We have a speaker coming to discuss new methods of varnish repair."

"Really." Piper didn't have a clue what that meant. "Sounds…"

"Tedious? Sleep-inducing?" He chuckled, cutting off any chance of her arguing otherwise. "I understand. I'm sure I would feel the same way about a lecture on flaky pastry. What about you? What are your plans for the evening?"

"You mean other than looking up John Allen on the internet? Nothing unusual. Do the cleaning I missed today, stream a little American television on my computer…"

"You should go out."

Piper shook her head. Clearly he was only saying that to be polite. They both knew she had no social life. The suggestion was as silly as her suggesting he stick around the house more. "I don't think so."

"Why not? Surely your culinary school friends…"

It was instinctive. As soon as he mentioned the word *friends*, she stiffened. "Culinary school isn't the kind of place where you make friends," she said. No sense hiding the reaction. "It's too competitive."

"You're surprised?"

"No. And yes." She struggled to explain. If the never-ending competition was the only problem, school wouldn't be so bad. "I guess I hoped that even with the competition, people would be friendlier. Supportive.

"Naive, I know," she added before he could say it. "I should have realized, school is school. Some things don't change."

"I don't understand. What does being at school have to do with anything?"

Of course he wouldn't understand. How could he?

"Were you popular in school?" she asked.

She watched as he contemplated the question. That he had to stop and think was almost an answer in itself. "I never paid attention to whether I was or not."

Bet he was, then. People who were well-liked never paid attention.

"And you were not popular?"

"I was chubby, poor and being raised by my sister." *Who stripped for a living*, she added silently. "Plus I caught lice in fifth grade. You can guess where that put me on the popularity scale."

"Where were your parents?"

"My mom died when I was little."

"I'm sorry."

"Happens."

Piper hated the sympathy in his voice. Pity parties were one thing, but to have others feeling pity for her...that only made her pathetic. "Needless to say, I was always a bit of an outsider."

Frederic nodded, attention on the space in front of him. "Personally, I always found being on my own to be the easier path," he said. "Being involved only means more drama."

"Oh, there was drama anyway." She didn't

mean to say anything aloud, the words just came out, so when he frowned, she did her best to play the comment off. "I mean, you know how kids can get."

She should have known he wouldn't let her get away with it. "What did they do?" he asked.

"Do? Nothing really. They mostly said stuff." *Hey, Piper, I got twenty bucks. Think your sister will give me a lap dance?* She winced at the memory. "That's how school works. Once you get a reputation, you're stuck with it. I learned to suck it up over time."

"Suck it up?"

"Cope," she said, translating the slang.

"Ah. I know what that is like."

Of course he would. He had his own issues, and they were far more serious than being teased in school. In a way it was funny, how they were both more alone than not. Piper wasn't sure why, but that made her like him all the more.

A very dangerous feeling.

"I'm making it sound worse than it was," she

told him, hoping to break the spell. "To be honest, I don't know why I brought high school up in the first place. We were talking about culinary school, which is supposed to be competitive, right? People are fighting for their livelihoods.

"Besides..." She went back to examining imaginary wrinkles. "It's not like I came to Paris to make friends."

Frederic leaned forward and knocked on the glass that divided them from the driver. "Michel," he said. "Would you pull over at the next stoplight?"

"Are you getting out?" They must have arrived at his meeting. That she knew he had a prior engagement didn't stop her stomach from dropping with insecurity.

"No," Frederic replied, "*we* are."

CHAPTER FOUR

THAT WAS POSSIBLY one of the weakest lies Frederic had ever heard, and Frederic had heard a lot of them. *Did not come here to make friends, indeed.*

He slid his hand along the door panel until his fingers curved around the handle. Blasted poor lighting made seeing details difficult. "We are going to see Paris," he said, letting daylight in.

"What are you talking about?"

"This is the second time you've mentioned Paris disappointing you. I refuse to let you think my city is cold and unfriendly."

Stepping onto the sidewalk, he motioned for her to do the same before scanning his surroundings to determine his location. Took only a moment before he managed to spy the Louvre's familiar Pyramide to his left. Perfect.

"We're going to walk a bit," he told Michel. "I will call you when we're ready to go home."

"What about your meeting?" Piper had joined him on the sidewalk. Her dress was ridiculously bright, much like the sun-filled sidewalk. The color filled his view every time he looked in her direction. He liked it. It was like looking into sunlight. It was not a color that should be lonely.

He stepped back so he could see more of her face. "The society will live without me. Defending our city's honor is far more important."

"You really don't have to do this."

"Don't I?" He started down the sidewalk, forcing her to catch up.

"But I thought you said Americans have unrealistic expectations about Paris."

"Yes, but that was before."

"Before what?"

Before he heard her trying so hard to sound casual about her loneliness. Perhaps it was the resignation in her voice, as though she didn't expect to have better. A tone that sounded suspiciously like the voices from his childhood. *Don't complain. Don't need.* The lessons he'd learned hurt when he heard them applied to someone else.

Or perhaps it was simply because he himself had only so long to appreciate his surroundings. Either way, he was suddenly gripped with the urge to show her more.

"Before I realized you spent your evenings inside streaming American television," he told her.

"I watch French shows, too."

He shot her a look. "Paris is a city meant to be experienced, not watched from the sidelines like a spectator. No wonder you have been disappointed. I bet you took one of those double-decker tour buses as well."

"What's wrong with that? You get to see all the important landmarks in one trip."

"Would you enjoy a gourmet meal in one bite?"

Her resulting silence told him she didn't have a counterargument. Smiling to himself, Frederic continued walking, his focus on the sidewalk unfolding in front of him. The *click-clack* of Piper's heels on the concrete made a pleasant rhythm for counting out steps.

"If we're going to the Louvre, I've already been," she said when they passed a street sign. "The bus stopped there. I even went in and waited in line to see the *Mona Lisa*."

It was amusing, the way she insisted on defending her tour. "I'm glad. I hope you saw some of the other great works as well. We are not going to the Louvre, however."

"Where are we going, then?"

"You will see."

Based on her exasperated sigh, Frederic could only imagine her expression. She probably rolled her eyes dramatically the way one of his students might.

"Don't you like surprises?" he asked.

"Only when I know what they are."

"Well, this time you'll simply have to trust me."

Having reached a cross street, he turned his

head. They stood too close for him to see her entire face, but in scanning, he saw that she was worrying her bottom lip. The pink flesh was pinched tight beneath her teeth.

"It's nothing bad, I promise," he told her. Then, because he could not stand to see that lip gnawed red, he reached out and cupped her cheek. Instantly, her lips parted with a tiny gasp of surprise. He lifted his eyes to meet hers. "Trust me."

"I—I do."

Frederic could feel curve of her earlobe teasing his fingertips. Without thinking, he brushed his little finger along the patch behind her ear. The skin beneath his hand was still cool from the car's air-conditioning and smooth as satin.

Her jaw muscle pulsed against his palm, making him realize what he was doing. "Good," he said, pulling his hand back. "Because we're almost there."

Resisting a suddenly inexplicable urge to grab her hand, he started across the street.

* * *

There turned out to be the Musée de l'Orangerie
in the Jardin des Tuileries, a smaller museum a
block away from the Louvre. Piper gasped as
she stepped through the vestibule. The room she
entered was all white, with soft light that turned
the color smooth as cream. A beautiful canvas of
a room created specifically for one purpose. To
display the panels that covered its walls.

"Monet's *Nymphéas*," Frederic said. "As it was
meant to be displayed."

The water lilies. Piper stepped toward the center of the room. A sea of color surrounded her.
Blues, greens, purples. She was swimming in
them.

"This is way better than a poster," she whispered. The room called for sounds no louder.

"I had a feeling you would like it."

"Like it? It's amazing."

"I'm glad you think so."

His breath tickled her ear, causing Piper to
brush at the sensation. In doing so, her fingers

accidently traced the same spot Frederic had touched when he cupped her cheek. Goose bumps danced across her skin. She rubbed her arms, chasing them away.

"I read about this museum when I was planning my trip." She forgot about it, though, once she realized visiting museums on her own wasn't much fun.

"It's one of my favorite places," Frederic told her.

Piper went back to studying the panels filling the room. They were larger than the painting she'd seen in Boston. These paintings loomed over her, dwarfing their surroundings with their magnitude.

"That's because they are murals," Frederic replied when she said as much. "This building was built specifically to house them."

"They're immense. I wonder how long it took to paint each panel?"

"I am guessing a very long time."

"Is that your expert opinion?"

"It is indeed." His grin was warm and endearing. If they were different people, Piper might think he was flirting.

Being late afternoon, most of the tourists had already filed through, leaving the two of them with the room to themselves. Frederic took a seat on the benches in the center of the room. "Monet has always been my favorite of the Impressionists," he said. "Did you know he painted over two hundred and fifty versions of his lily pond? Many of them he painted while he had cataracts. You can tell which ones because they have red in them."

"Is that why you like him?"

"You mean, do I feel some sort of affinity for him because we both have bad eyes?" He shrugged. "Never thought much about it. But now that you ask, I suppose I do have a unique appreciation for what he accomplished."

Piper joined him on the bench, her legs stretched in the opposite direction from his. "Did you ever think of becoming an artist?" All the art talk the

past couple days had made her curious. His interest in art history had to start somewhere. Was it
the backup for a different goal? It would be nice
to know if someone else stumbled while chasing a dream.

It was hard to picture Frederic failing at anything, though…

"I dabbled a little when I was younger. I'm not
sure you'd call the results art."

"Worse than the painting Bernard tried to sell
you?"

God, she liked his laugh. It sounded so rich and
throaty, even when soft. "Don't let Bernard hear
you say that," he said. "And yes, it was worse. For
the record, the Biskup was not a bad painting."

"No, just depressing."

"Some people like depressing art. As for my
abilities…I'm afraid the artistic gene stopped
with my mother."

"So your mother was an artist. Do you have
any of her paintings?" The floral one in the salon,
she bet.

"Unfortunately, no. She had to give up her work."

"Why?"

His gaze dropped to the floor. "She just did."

Not by choice, either, she'd say, based on the sorrow in his voice. What happened? She wanted to ask, but it was obvious Frederic didn't want to share and who was she to push? After all, there were things in her life she wasn't ready to share either. She settled for giving his shoulder a nudge to draw him back to the moment. "So your lack of an art gene... Is that why you became a teacher? Because those who can't, teach?"

If ever a comment didn't fit a person. Fortunately, Frederic got the joke and nudged her shoulder in return. "Professor, thank you very much. There's a second set of panels in the next room. Then I want to take you upstairs to see another favorite of mine. If you're a good girl, we can stop at the gift shop and buy you a new poster as well."

"Don't let Bernard hear you say that," Piper

shot back with a smirk. She was holding him to that promise, though.

Piper assumed that once they finished at L'Orangerie, Frederic would call for the car so they could return to the house, but he did not. Instead, he asked her for the time.

"Almost half past six," Piper replied.

"Good. We have plenty of time."

"Plenty of time for what?"

"To walk along the river, of course. We'll walk until we get hungry, and then we'll find a place to eat."

"You don't have to take me to dinner," she told him.

"Why not? You can tell me if the food holds up to your culinary school standards."

"Because…" Because she hadn't forgotten that she was talking about her sad, friendless state just before he stopped the car, which made her fear this adventure was nothing more than a very romantic pity trip. "I've already taken up too much of your day as it is." Along with half of yesterday too. "I'm sure you've got other things you'd rather do."

"I already told you, I do not. What I do want is to enjoy this beautiful summer night."

Taking her by the elbow, he stepped off the curb only to jump back when a car horn blared loudly.

"Perhaps we should wait until the light changes." He spoke with a smile, but Piper saw a pair of pink spots peering out beneath the rims of his aviators nonetheless. "I'm usually quite good about checking traffic, but sometimes I get distracted."

"I didn't look, either," she pointed out. "We both deserved the horn in this case."

Even so, the incident must have bothered Frederic more than he let on, because once they were across the street, he fell quiet.

Once again, Piper didn't push. People needed to work out their embarrassment their own way, even people like Frederic, who didn't get embarrassed all that often. As they walked in silence, she contented herself with studying the riverbank. The bag carrying her posters from L'Orangerie slapped against her thigh, and she imagined the sound was the water lapping the river's edge.

The view was a familiar one. Over the past eight months, Piper had walked the river dozens of times. After school. On errands. In all four seasons. Yesterday, if someone had asked her, she would have said the path didn't live up to the billing... Today, though... Today, it was as though she was seeing the riverbanks for the first time. Probably because she wasn't walking alone.

More than that. For the first time in months, she didn't *feel* alone.

Looking over at Frederic, she wondered how many of the people passing them envied her his company. A man who so obviously could have his pick of any woman in Paris. Her insides toppled end over end that she was the one he picked. So what if today was a pity date? Tomorrow's routine would return soon enough. Today she would take his pity, and enjoy the break.

"My mother."

Frederic's voice was soft and unexpected. Yanked from her thoughts, Piper nearly stumbled.

"You asked me why I studied art history," he said. "My mother was the one who taught me to appreciate art."

Strange that he would choose now to address a remark made at the museum. Here she thought he'd been dwelling on their near miss with the car. Unless the two were related.

"Sounds like you got part of the art gene after all," she said.

"More likely she wanted to make sure I was exposed to as many beautiful things as possible."

There, Piper realized sadly, was the link. She had this image of Frederic's mother exposing him to sight after sight. How young had he been when his eyes started to fail? "It's funny," she heard herself saying, "but sometimes I forget you have trouble seeing. You certainly wouldn't know it at home."

"That is because I work hard to make sure I function without assistance. I made up my mind very early in life that blindness wouldn't leave me helpless."

"You're not blind, though."

"Yet."

Her stomach sank. In the back of her mind, she'd known what his response would be, but she'd hoped otherwise. "I'm sorry."

"Don't be," he said cutting her off. "I accepted my fate a long time ago. Someday, I will wake up and my eyesight will be gone. Perhaps not so drastically, but it will happen."

"What will you do then?" Piper wasn't sure she wanted to know. There was a resignation to his voice that made her sad.

Frederic stopped so he could turn to face her. The sunglasses masked his eyes, but the rest of his face was resolute. "I will deal."

A fair enough answer. Why then did it make

her want to throw her arms around him and hold on tight?

"If my sister were here, she'd add, 'then figure out a way to fix the situation'."

His mouth curved into a smile. "Somehow I doubt she was referring to degenerative eye disease."

"No, although she definitely got us out of some dark times."

"Dark?"

Probably not the best word to use. Giving a shrug, she started to do what she always did and play off the comment, but then changed her mind. "Things weren't always great when I was growing up. Patience always did her best to make them better. I owe her everything." A small wedge of guilt worked its way into her throat, the way it always did when talking about her sister.

"Sounds like your sister is a special woman."

"I always thought so," she said.

"Must run in the family."

Was he talking about her? Piper shook her head. "I don't think…"

He pressed a finger to her lips. "Never turn down a compliment, Piper."

What was it with Frederic touching her and walking away? Twice now his fingers had stroked her face. She traced the spot on her lips, convinced his fingers left a part of himself behind. Why else would they continue to tingle?

"Piper?" Ahead a few feet, Frederic had stopped and was looking for her.

"Sorry, I was think— Do I hear music?"

She did. The soft sound of violins and accordians could be heard in the distance.

"It's coming from around the bend," Frederic said.

"A concert?" It sounded like too many instruments to be a regular sidewalk performance. A dinner cruise maybe. She tried to remember if there was a dock ahead.

Meanwhile, Frederic was trying very hard to hide a smile. "You know what it is, don't you?"

"Perhaps," he replied.

Oh, he definitely knew. He was holding out on her, just like he did with the Monet exhibit. Question was, what was he hiding? A thrill of anticipation passed through her, strengthened by her still-tingling lips. They rounded the corner, and she spied a large crowd surrounding the amphitheaters. "It *is* a concert."

"Is it? You might want to look closer." He flashed another one of those mysterious smiles, making Piper think her insides might melt.

Drawing closer, she saw that the crowd was watching a swirl of movement. "Oh my God, are they dancing?"

"Ballroom dancing at dusk," Frederic murmured in her ear. "A summer tradition."

It was a beautiful sight to see. Dozens of couples twirling to the music.

Piper pointed to a graceful blonde woman moving between the dance groups. "The woman in the red shirt. Is she a judge or something?"

"Instructor, more likely. Here to help the less-skilled dancers learn the steps."

Didn't look as if anyone needed lessons. The pairs moved in graceful synchronicity to the slow, pulsing beat. "Do you know what dance they are performing?"

"Based on the music, I would say the tango."

She should have known. The air was ripe with sensuality. You could literally feel the passion as the more experienced dancers stalked the dance floor. Piper felt her breath quickening in response. Behind her, Frederic breathed quickly as well, his chest brushing against her back with each rise and fall of his lungs. A dinner boat passed, its bow lights creating a fairy-tale background just as the music peaked.

"Wow," she whispered when the song had ended. She looked over her shoulder. "I've never really seen ballroom dancing up close before. It's beautiful to watch."

A new song began to play. Piper recognized the strands of "La Vie en Rose."

"The dancing is open to everyone," Frederic said. "Would you like to join them?"

"Out there? I'm no ballroom dancer."

"You don't have to be. The only requirement is to enjoy moving to the music."

More couples were making their way to the dance floor, made brave by the familiar music. Piper couldn't help noticing that several of the pairings barely moved. They were content to simply hold each other and sway to the beat.

She imagined Frederic's arms holding her and grew warm all over. Before she could say a word, a hand molded to the small of her back and she was propelled forward.

"Stay by the edge, where there isn't too much of a crowd," he said. Piper really wished his breath wouldn't tease her skin the way it did.

He led her to an open space near where they were standing. "I hope you can do this without stepping on anyone's toes, because I can't," she said.

His arm slipped around her waist and pulled

her tight. "Moving to the music is the easy part," he told her. "It's the crowds that are the problem."

The crowds, she repeated to herself. The crowds were why he was holding her so close. Another inch or so, and her cheek would be flush with his shoulder. The music's familiar three-beat rhythm echoed in her ear. Head bobbing in time, Piper counted her steps. "Relax," he said. His chest rumbled against her cheek as he spoke. "Let the music guide your feet."

"I think my feet might be tone-deaf."

"Nonsense. You're in Paris. Everyone is graceful in Paris." He tightened his grip, his cheek pressing against her temple. "Let yourself go and enjoy."

Why not? When would she ever have this opportunity again? The sun was setting, the breeze was warm and the spires of Notre Dame were keeping watch. What could be more magical? Piper closed her eyes and let the music take control. It couldn't have been more perfect.

* * *

"See?" Frederic said. "I told you that you could dance."

Truthfully, they weren't so much dancing as swaying in time, but Frederic didn't mind. The crowd made more complex moves difficult for him. Holding Piper's hand against his chest, he contented himself with inhaling the scent drifting off her skin. How was it a woman could smell so good without perfume?

Piper had her head nestled against his shoulder, the crown of her head tucked near his chin. He wondered if she realized how much like an embrace their dance had become. Not that he was averse to the position. It had been a while since he held a beautiful woman so close. And he couldn't remember the last time he actually danced with a woman.

"Hold me close and hold me fast," Piper was singing under her breath. "The magic spell you cast."

"This is *la vie en rose*," he finished.

She lifted her head and they were close enough that he could see the dreamy expression in her eyes. The soft glow brought his awareness to life.

"I always loved this song," she told him. "Before I came here, I used to imagine the city with accordion players on all the streets playing this song, just so people could walk around to it."

She really did have a romantic's view of his city. Shame on those other students for destroying that dream. "I'm sorry we let you down."

"It's okay," she said, putting her head back on his shoulder. "This works, too."

They walked the rest of the way home. He would probably regret using his eyes so much, but at the moment, listening to Piper hum "La Vie en Rose" under her breath, he thought it worth the sacrifice.

Ahead, the Eiffel Tower blinked in all its lit-up glory. Frederic couldn't help but stop. "Beautiful, isn't it?" he said.

"Yeah, it is," she said, craning her neck to get a

better view. "No matter how cranky I get about life in Paris, I can never hate the tower."

Neither could he. He didn't know why, but he found himself feeling very open and poetic to-night. Wasn't like him. As a rule, he preferred to keep the world at arm's length. He never wanted to get to a point where someone felt obligated to him because they shared a closeness. He knew only too well what obligation led to. Far easier—and safer—to stay charming and superficial. To-night, though, it seemed he was destined to break that rule.

"I told myself a long time ago that I would never take the tower for granted," he told Piper. "Ever since then, I've made a point of looking at her every day."

Because you never know when you'll have the chance to see it again.

He heard a soft cough. Turning his head, he saw Piper smiling at him. "Thank you," she said. "For this afternoon. For showing me the Paris I've always dreamed of. I'll never forget it."

Frederic didn't know what to say. He still wasn't 100 percent sure why she compelled him to be so whimsical. Inexplicable as his decision was, however, he had to admit that she wasn't the only one who'd enjoyed the day. "I'm glad," he said. "I had a good time, too."

She was smiling, and he could make out a sparkle shimmering in her eyes. Their sheen was luminescent. So was her skin, he thought, letting his eyes take in as much as they were able. The smell of vanilla and spices wafted toward him, like a siren's call. Then suddenly, she was closer, and her lips brushed his cheek in a shy kiss.

The feel of her lips on him stayed long after Piper disappeared into her rooms. Not yet ready to head upstairs, Frederic sat in the dark and studied his tower. Today was not what he expected. Piper wasn't what he expected.

Whether or not that was a good thing, he didn't know.

CHAPTER FIVE

IT WAS OFFICIAL. Piper hated Chef Despelteau as much as he hated her. There was no way her culinary skills were that far below the rest of the class. Honestly, she was beginning to think the man would have a problem with Julia Child's French cooking.

Wonder what Chef Despelteau would think if he knew she didn't like half the foods they were preparing? They were all so froufrou.

Feeling rebellious, she stopped at the grocery on her way home and bought a roast and potatoes. She'd like to see Chef Despelteau make a Yankee pot roast as well as she could.

Might as well face it, babe, you're a common food girl at heart. A common girl, period.

Maybe so, but she was also a girl who had

waltzed under the Paris moon. How many people back home could say that? No sooner did the
thought enter her head than the memory washed
over her. Piper smiled. If she concentrated, she
could remember every detail, right down to the
smell of Frederic's skin.

So many of the guys she knew used slow dancing as an excuse to cop a feel. They'd rest their
hands on your rear or plaster their bodies so
tightly against yours that the two of you might as
well be sleeping together. Frederic held a woman
like a man who had nothing to prove. Of course,
it didn't matter how he held her. It wasn't as if
last night was like some magic spell that changed
them from boss and employee into something
else.

Still, he'd given her a great memory. Now if
anyone asked, she wouldn't have to lie about having spent time with a handsome Frenchman.

She arrived at the house to find her handsome
Frenchman stretched out in his chair again.
Amazing how he could make something as

simple as sprawling in a chair look elegant. He had one arm flung over his eyes while the other rested gently on his stomach. Piper's gaze fell to the long fingers that were curled ever so slightly against his shirt. As though it remembered their touch, her skin began to tingle.

"I know you're standing there," he said, stirring.

Piper winced at getting caught. Thank goodness she was behind the chair so he couldn't see how red her cheeks were.

"I thought I might have to wake you up again," she said. "You looked dead to the world."

"Only resting. My meeting for tonight had been canceled, so I decided to rest my eyes for a moment. They tend to get tired this time of day."

"Sorry I disturbed you then." It never occurred to her, what with his limited field of vision, how much energy it must take for him to focus. Making yesterday's adventure all the more special.

"No worries. Are you carrying something?"

She held up the brightly colored bag she used for errands. "Ahh, I thought I saw a pink handle."

"Groceries. I decided to make a pot roast." Piper paused. If his meeting was canceled, did that mean he would be home for dinner?

"Will that be a problem?" Frederic asked when she checked.

Before today, she would have said no. While Frederic's schedule kept him out of the house most nights, there were times when he stayed home and expected her to cook. All those nights happened before they'd danced together, however. Those few minutes in his arms had colored their relationship. An ordinary activity such as cooking now had a more intimate flavor.

But the inability to separate last night and today was her problem, wasn't it? When push came to shove, Frederic was still her boss and she still his housekeeper.

Offering a smile, she replied in as casual a voice as she could muster. "Why would it be a problem? Cooking is part of my job, isn't it? I mean, the title is housekeeper-slash-cook."

"Yes, but when I mentioned staying in, your voice sounded a little...off. Made me concerned."

"I was calculating cooking times in my head is all. To make sure I don't serve you too late." *Please don't ask what time I consider late because I'm totally making things up.*

"You don't have to worry about the time. I'll eat whenever the meal is ready."

"Well, I better go change uniforms and get started. Oh, by the way," she said, remembering. "I called the carpet cleaning company. They're closed for vacation. I made a note to call them next week."

"That's not necessary, you know."

"It is if you want to get rid of the coffee stain."

"No, I mean, changing. You don't have to switch uniforms on my account."

"You might change your mind when you realize how badly this jacket smells like today's seafood lesson."

"I meant you don't have to wear a uniform. Put on your regular clothes."

But she always wore a uniform. The employment agency insisted. *To maintain a barrier between staff and the house* or something like that.

"I've been thinking about it for a couple days. There is no reason you should have to keep changing from one uniform to another and back every day. You should be comfortable."

Comfortable while cooking for him. Yeah, that wouldn't feel domestic at all. "Thanks," she told him. "I'll do that."

A short while later, the kitchen smelled like beef and onions. Piper breathed in the familiar scents to calm her nerves. *Get a grip*, she told herself. *It's no different from any other night.* In fact, this was a good reminder to keep her head on straight. As her little stare-fest in the living room proved, she was crossing the line from attractive boss to being attracted to her boss—something neither of them needed.

Her attention shifted to the phone on the counter. Odd. She had two missed calls. She must have been so engrossed in chopping vegetables she didn't notice the phone vibrating. Both were from Patience. Wanting to know how the painting search was going, no doubt. Piper wasn't going to have much to tell her. John Allen hadn't returned her phone call yet.

Only, Patience's voice mail wasn't about the painting. It was about her and Stuart Duchenko. She replayed the message twice to make sure she heard her sister correctly. Difficult, since Patience was sniffling throughout.

Oh, Patience. Sick to her stomach, she dropped into one of the kitchen chairs and stared at the call screen. You'd think after everything else, her sister would catch a break.

"I can smell dinner from up in my office. It smells delicious."

"Thanks," she replied, attention stuck on the phone. She didn't even bother to look up when Frederic joined her.

"Something has upset you." His arm reached across the table and brushed the top of her wrist, drawing her attention. "Is it about the painting? Did Monsieur Allen have bad news?"

"No, I'm still waiting to hear from him. My sister left her job." Her thumb wavered between texting and calling direct. Video chatting would be best, but she didn't know if Patience had her laptop.

Frederic drew up a chair and sat down. "She is no longer working for Ana Duchenko? Why not? I was under the impression she cared about the woman."

"She does. Problem is she cares about Stuart Duchenko more."

"The nephew who is searching for the painting. I didn't realize they were…friends."

Piper had to smile at his use of euphemisms. "According to her voice mail, they aren't 'friends' any longer. They had a fight about something in her past. She was crying, so I couldn't understand the whole message. I'll find out more when I call her back."

Piper's eyes dropped back to her phone screen. "And here I thought after everything she'd been through, she'd finally found happiness."

"Everything she'd been through? I don't understand. Yesterday you said you both suffered through tough times."

"We did. But Patience suffered more, or at least I think so."

"What do you mean?"

Piper exhaled. She hadn't planned on sharing the story with him, but now that she opened the door, she might as well walk all the way through. After all, Frederic opened up about his eyesight, right?

"Do you remember when I told you that no matter how tough life got for us, Patience found a way to make it better?"

"Yes."

"Well, life got real tough. Like the two of us living in a car tough."

She tried not to cringe at his sudden sharp breath. "You—you were homeless?"

"Only for a week or so." Yesterday's sympathy had returned to his voice. Hearing it left a sour taste in her mouth and so she rushed to erase it as quickly as possible. "It was right after my mom died. Soon as we could afford to, we found a cheap motel room and then later an apartment."

"Must have been terrifying."

"I was more scared someone would find out and take me away. Patience promised we would stay together."

"She kept her promise."

"Yes, she did. She took the only job she could find to pay the bills."

"Working for Ana Duchenko as a housekeeper."

"The job with Ana came later, after I moved here. When I was a kid, she was a dancer in a club. A club where women were paid to dance."

There was a pause as the full meaning of her answer sank in. "I see," he said finally.

"She didn't have a choice." The defense came automatically, before he could say anything judgmental. "I told you, it was the first job she could find."

Twirling her phone end over end, she thought about those dark days. Remembering how she sat shivering in a blanket in the backseat, crying because the only thing she'd eaten that day were the free saltines they swiped from the local convenience store. "For most of my life it's been just me and Patience. Couldn't have been easy being stuck raising a kid right out of high school."

"I would think it was hard for both of you."

He spoke frankly, exactly the way Piper preferred. Bluntness was so much better than pity or sarcasm.

"When she first got the job I was too young to understand what she was doing," she told him. "Then when I was old enough…" Hopefully, her shrug filled in the blanks. When she was old enough, she sucked it up, for Patience's sake.

"The argument your sister and the Duchenko

nephew had? This is the information he discovered?"

"I think he learned a few of the more sordid details. From the sound of it, there were things I didn't even know about."

It made her wonder how many more difficulties her sister bore alone for Piper's sake. The guilt she carried on her shoulders pressed heavier.

Meanwhile, Frederic sat stiffly in his chair, drawing patterns on the table with his index finger. "Sounds as if both of you were very brave. I've known people who weren't half as brave when life kicked them."

Who? Certainly not him.

"If your sister is as strong as she sounds," he continued, "then I am sure she will weather this storm as well. Did you not just say she always found a way to fix a bad situation?"

"You're right. She did." Patience was a survivor. A fact Piper needed to remember. "Being over five thousand miles away has got me on edge. I'm sure that once I have a chance to talk with her, I'll feel better."

In fact, her spirits were already beginning to lift, in large part because of the man across from her. "Who knows? Maybe once he's had a chance to get over the shock, Stuart will realize Patience's past is no big deal." After all, life has a way of doing a one-eighty on you. Last week she would have been sitting here dealing with Patience's message on her own.

"Thank you," she said.

"For what?"

"Listening. It was nice having a shoulder for a change." Reaching across the table, she covered his hand with hers. It was a simple gesture, meant to be an expression of gratitude, but it sent warmth coiling through Piper in unexpected ways. She looked up, wondering if Frederic noticed her reaction, and saw that his eyes were dark with an unreadable emotion. Her pulse skipped.

"I should go call her back," she said, standing.

Her hand didn't seem to want to separate from his; she had to force the command down her arm to make it move. "I'll try to be quick."

"Take as much time as you'd like," Frederic told her. His attention was on the hand she had just released, his voice distracted.

Piper didn't want to think about it. Pushing the moment from her thoughts, she headed toward her suite, her finger hitting redial before she reached it. Patience's phone went straight to voice mail. "You can't call me crying, then not answer your phone," she said. "Call me back ASAP. Everything will be okay," she added in a gentle voice.

Barely two seconds went by before a message appeared on her screen.

Doing better. Checking into a motel. Will call u later.

Soon, OK? Piper typed back. Love you.

Her sister would bounce back, Piper reminded herself as she tucked the phone in her back pocket. Frederic was right about her being a survivor. It still sucked though that Patience couldn't seem to catch any happiness.

Maybe it wasn't in the Rush girl DNA. What with them being common girls and all that, maybe they weren't meant to be anything more. She tapped the phone against her lips. At least Piper was here making sure some of her sister's sacrifices were worthwhile.

A thought came to her. There was one more thing she could do. She could talk to Stuart herself. Piper opened her email.

Frederic was moving about the kitchen when she returned a short time later. Whatever the thickness was that had been in the atmosphere before she left had eased. "Did you talk to your sister?" he asked.

"No, but she texted me. Said she's feeling better."

"You seem to be, as well."

Yeah, she was. "That's because after I heard

from Patience, I decided to take a page from her playbook and do something to fix the situation. I decided to contact Stuart to see if I could make him see how backed in a corner Patience was back then."

"Good thinking."

"Unnecessary too. When I logged on, I found an email from him asking how he could make things right."

Might not be perfect, but it was a start.

"There you go. He's already over whatever news he learned. I'm sure that means they will talk things out."

"I really hope so."

All of sudden she saw that Frederic was setting the kitchen table. With two place settings.

"I thought we'd be more comfortable in here," he said when he noticed her staring.

"We're eating together?" All the other times she'd served him, he'd eaten in the dining room.

"Foolish for us to eat in separate rooms, is it not? Especially now that we are friends."

Friends. Apparently, he forgot that he used the same term to describe Patience's and Stuart's relationship.

She watched as he moved from cupboard to table. She never noticed before, but he looked at the space in sections, presumably until the object he was seeking came into view. Methodical, but subtle and graceful at the same time. To the unknowing eye, he was simply a man in supreme control. Heck, he looked that way to her *knowing* eye. She couldn't imagine him being anything but in control.

What was it she was supposed to remember about finding him attractive and being attracted?

"...going?"

He was looking in her direction waiting for an answer. "Should I assume from your lack of response that class did not go well again today?"

Right, he was talking about school. Piper shook her head. "No, but school never does go well, so it's no big deal."

"I am sorry." His voice lifted at the end, as if he wasn't sure he should offer condolences or not.

"Hey, like I said yesterday, great cooking is an art. Don't all artists suffer?"

"Some do."

"Well, so do some chefs. I'm telling myself that in the end, the hassle is making me a better chef.

"In the meantime," she said, reaching for the cornstarch, "I'm learning a whole bunch of new ways to insult a person's dinner. Today's word was *mundane*. My sauce was mundane. I like to think it's a step up from earlier this week when my food was uninspired."

"I see your teacher is one of those instructors."

"What do you mean, 'one of those'?" she asked as she mixed thickener for the gravy.

"I mean the type who believes insulting their students makes for good motivation."

"Assuming he is trying to motivate and not simply telling the truth."

"The aromas in this kitchen suggest otherwise."

It felt so good to have someone compliment

her cooking, Piper decided to not worry about whether he was being polite and smiled instead. "Pot roast is one of my specialties. I've always been wicked good when it comes to New England cooking. Your country…" She waved her hand back and forth. "Not so much. I should have realized after I tried to make vichyssoise." Good Lord, she hadn't thought about that in ages. The memory made her laugh. "I think I was seven."

"And attempting French cooking?"

"What can I say? I was a prodigy." She left out the part about how if she didn't cook, she didn't eat. "Anyway, someone mentioned cold potato soup on TV. I figured it couldn't be that hard to make, so I tried it. Ended up serving Patience a can of condensed potato soup straight out of the cupboard. No water or anything." She could imagine what Chef Despelteau would say.

"I'm glad your skills improved."

"Me, too. And for the record, I know how to make a kick-ass vichyssoise now. Patience refuses to eat it, though. Can't really blame her. Too many canned soup dinners burned her out."

Piper stared at the cloudy liquid in front of her. "She's the reason I'm here, you know. In Paris. She never stopped encouraging me. Telling me I could do anything I wanted."

"Like a good parent should."

"She'd laugh if she heard you say that, but yeah, exactly like a parent. I remember when I got my acceptance letter. She was more excited than I was." There was no way Piper couldn't fulfill their dream after that.

Distracted by memories, Piper forgot she was supposed to be stirring the thickener. The bowl slipped from her hands, bounced off the counter edge and landed on the floor.

Shoot. Cornstarch splattered the cabinets. That's what she got for not paying attention. She reached for the paper towels only to collide with Frederic as he did the same. Their fingers linked together.

Just like that, the thickness returned to the atmosphere. Piper felt it pressing around them, like energy waiting to hum. She looked at their interlocked fingers and wondered why neither of them had pulled away.

"Guess this is the week for spills," she joked.

"This is the week for a lot of broken rules," he said, a strangely serious response to what was meant as a tension breaker. She'd been looking for something to distract from the pull of attraction gathering strength in her belly. Piper didn't have to look up to know Frederic felt similarly. They were both breathing faster. Out of the corner of her eye, she saw his head dip closer, intentions clear. If she said no, he would stop.

She met him halfway.

Their mouths slid together as easily as their hands. Piper sighed at how well they fit. Frederic kissed like he moved, each caress of his lips deliberate and sure. His hand still gripping hers, he wrapped his other arm around her waist and pulled her close. *Just like dancing,* she thought as her eyes fluttered shut.

A moment later, Frederic broke away. Shaking and out of breath, Piper leaned her forehead against his. Holy cow! Never in a million years did she think a kiss could feel like that.

Frederic looked shell-shocked himself. She took pleasure in seeing his hand shake as he swiped a thumb across her lower lip. "Your phone is ringing," he said in a tight voice.

Phone? Piper blinked. Sure enough, she heard the sound of computerized jazz coming from her pocket. "Th-that's probably Patience."

"You should answer."

Yes, she should. Balling the hand Frederic had been holding into a fist, she reached for the phone with her other.

Not Patience. The number on her call screen was unfamiliar. She didn't know if they had telemarketers in France, but if this was one, she was not going to hang up politely.

"Hello!" a cheery voice replied. "Am I speaking with Piper Rush? This is John Allen. I understand you're interested in a painting of mine."

* * *

While Piper spoke to John Allen, Frederic moved across the room. He needed to put some space between them before he took his housekeeper on the kitchen floor. It wasn't that he was against making love in the kitchen; he simply wasn't sure he should make love to Piper. As she was quickly proving, Piper was no ordinary housekeeper. She was soft and sweet in ways he wasn't used to. There was an essence about her that demanded connection, compelling him to reach out to her. She made him want to comfort her.

She… God, she tasted like vanilla. She made him want to taste her again. But was that a good idea?

Just then, Piper laughed, a sweet sound that reminded him of tinkling crystal, and he thought, perhaps it was a very good idea.

"Are you sure?" he heard her ask. "That would be great. Miss Duchenko would be thrilled."

Thrilled at what? Curiosity overrode his desire. Did this mean Allen had the painting? That they had tracked down the work so easily was almost comical. Experts searched lifetimes for paintings and sculptures and here his houskeeper locates one in three days? Amazing.

He was surprised at his investment in the search. Naturally, he would have a passing interest in tracking down a lost painting of any kind, even a scandalous portrait by a no-name artist like this one. The fact that his interest ran deeper he attributed to his frighteningly intriguing housekeeper.

"Looks like I'm going to England on an art hunt after all," Piper announced when she hung up. "Mr. Allen has invited me to see *Ana Reclining* in person."

"Congratulations." Her smile was contagious. "Does his invitation mean he is willing to part with the painting?"

"He said he would have to think about whether he was willing to sell. The painting is one of his favorite pieces."

But of course it was. As anyone hoping to net a good price would say.

"However, he did offer to let me inspect the painting's condition and to take a photograph of the work for Ana. If he doesn't sell, she will at least have proof one of her portraits survived."

Explaining why Miss Duchenko would be thrilled.

"I thought I would go this weekend. Mr. Allen's leaving on a business trip next week and wasn't sure how long he'd be gone. I figured I could take the train out tomorrow. That is, if you can spare me for a few days."

"I can," he replied. But did he want to? It was clear from the excited energy in her voice that the rest of tonight would be absorbed by itineraries and trip planning. To then have to wait an entire weekend before having the chance to kiss her again?

The words were out of his mouth before he had a chance to think them through. "Actually, I thought I would go with you."

"You did?"

"Why not? I've been part of your search for the last two days. Surely you didn't expect me to stay home when you got to the best part?"

"Do you really want to?" he heard her ask. "Go to England?"

"Yes, Piper, I do."

He could see her fidgeting as she tried to decide. After the kiss they just shared, there could be no doubt as to what traveling together to England might lead to. Frederic stayed quiet; he wouldn't push her one way or the other. No matter how tempting the thought of kissing her into agreement.

From her spot across the room, Piper nodded. "What time do you want to leave?"

CHAPTER SIX

PIPER WASN'T AN IDIOT. She knew perfectly well what could happen if Frederic accompanied her to England. Especially after the kiss they shared.

What she hadn't known was that kissing Frederic would leave her with some kind of ultra-hyper responsiveness that would fade. Every move, every sound Frederic made—right down to the crinkle of his shirt when he bent his elbow—sent a rush of awareness running through her. You'd think it was her first kiss. In a way, it was. It was certainly the first kiss that made her insides feel as though they were being kissed, too. If one short kiss could make her feel this way, she hated to think what would happen if he kissed without interruption.

The only thing that kept her from throwing

herself at him to find out was, ironically enough, arranging their trip.

They caught the first train the next morning.

Piper took out the map of England she'd bought at the station and located the town where John Allen lived. "Have you been to this place before?" she asked Frederic.

"The town? No. I've been to the Cotswolds several times, though."

As he answered, he shifted in his seat, causing his jeans leg to brush hers. Impossibly the contact managed to reach through the layers to leave goose bumps.

The hyperawareness was as strong as ever.

Piper shifted in her seat as well, hoping she could add a little space between their legs. Otherwise, it would be a very long tunnel ride. "I read about the Cotswolds online last night." Mainly because she needed to do something to calm the hyperawareness. Turned out reading up on the trip you were taking with the man who kissed you senseless wasn't a relaxing solution. "It looked gorgeous in the pictures." Not to mention romantic. Another reason she had trouble sleeping.

She suddenly wondered what kind of visits Frederic's other trips to the Cotswolds were. "Did you go there on vacation?"

"There's an abbey not far from Chipping Campden that has the most unique ninth-century mural of Saint Michael. I wrote a journal paper on it." There was nostalgia in his smile. "I heard they restored it a few years ago. I wonder how it turned out."

"Why don't we go see it while we're in the area?" As far as she was concerned, anything that put such a smile on his face had to be worth a visit.

"I was already planning to," he replied. "Did you know that for centuries, no one knew this mural was there? At some point, it was covered by a second layer of stone. It was discovered when a lightning strike knocked a piece of the outer wall loose."

"Do they know why it was covered up?"

"No one knows for sure. My personal theory is that it was hidden during the Reformation so as not to anger Henry VIII." He launched into an explanation about the monks and allegiance to the king only to stop suddenly with a blush. "Sorry. I'm afraid I get carried away."

"It's okay—I don't mind," Piper replied. She'd been only half listening anyway. Too busy enjoying the sparkle in his eyes. "I have to be honest," she told him. "It's hard to imagine you poring over books in a research library." Today, for example, in his jeans and silk T-shirt, he looked more like a vacationing playboy or professional soccer player.

"Sit in one of my classes sometime. My students will say I must spend all my time there. That is why my lectures are so boring."

"They are not." She could listen to him talk all day.

"You are in a rarefied group then. Sometimes I think it's a good thing my lecture hall has low lighting. Keeps me from seeing how many of my students have fallen asleep. It's difficult enough when I call on them and they can't repeat what I mentioned five minutes earlier."

He was exaggerating. Piper honestly couldn't see him as boring, no matter how dry the topic. Distracting, however, was a far different story. If she were a college student, she could see herself spending class time fantasizing about the professor. "Your classes wouldn't be mostly female, would they?"

"About a seventy to thirty percent ratio. Why?"

"Trust me, those girls aren't sleeping."

The blush creeping over his cheeks was as captivating as the rest of him. "Is that your way of suggesting they're captivated by my looks?"

Piper joined him in blushing. "Is that your way of fishing for a compliment?"

"Perhaps." He traced a pattern across the map with his index finger. Piper followed with her eyes, and wondered if he was drawing a route or tracing aimless lines.

"I could say the same for you as well," he murmured without looking up.

"That I'm fishing for compliments?"

"That it's easy to be distracted by your good looks."

"Says the man who can't see." Realizing what she said, Piper started to cringe, only to stop when Frederic let out a laugh.

"Even through a pinhole, a man can see a diamond."

"Now I know you're exaggerating."

"Only a little." He moved his tracing from the map to her arm, his finger following the same lazy, loopy path across her skin. "You are a beautiful woman."

Piper pushed back a shiver. "I bet you say that to all your housekeepers."

"Only the American ones."

"Let me guess, you only hire Americans."

"No. You are the first." His finger took one last trip down her arm and disappeared. "I don't make a habit of kissing the help."

"Then why…?" What made her so different? She wasn't used to being singled out as special.

"I don't know," Frederic replied. He looked past her for a moment as if trying to figure out the answer himself before smiling at her again. "Why don't we enjoy it for what it is?"

"What is it?"

"Today? It is a road trip."

"And tomorrow?"

"Why don't we take things as they come? Stay in the present."

In other words, no strings attached.

"When I was a little kid, living in the present meant we were sure we'd have enough rent money." It was meant to be a joke, but the catch in her voice killed the effect.

Frederic shifted so they were face-to-face and took her hand. "I don't believe in giving false expectations," he told her. "Especially when it comes to relationships. It wouldn't be fair."

For whom? The other day he said being involved only meant more drama. Was that what he feared? That she might grow too attached? If so, maybe he should work on being a little less charming and attractive.

"Maybe I'm old-fashioned, but I like to know what I'm getting into," she said, only to real-ize that he had told her in very clear terms. No strings.

"You're thinking too much. Let us take one moment at a time, all right? Whatever happens, happens. There is no pressure."

Piper nodded. No pressure she could do.

Hopefully.

There was a car and driver waiting for them when they arrived at Saint Pancras station. A girl could get pretty spoiled by this kind of travel, Piper decided as she slid into the backseat. Defi-nitely beat struggling to drive on the wrong side of the road with a rented stick shift. Which is what she'd be doing if Frederic weren't with her.

Best not to get too spoiled, though. At some point this whole Cinderella experience was going to end. There would be no limousines driving her around Boston. No guarantee she would have limousines driving her around Paris much, either. Taking things moment to moment could mean going back to being a housekeeper on Monday.

One good thing did come out of Frederic's "no pressure" comment, though. She managed to put the lid back on her over-boiling senses, meaning she could actually sit in the backseat without too much awareness. The only time she had real problems was when Frederic leaned into her space, sending a hint of his spicy wood aftershave in her direction. Then she would get a most unwelcome flutter below the waist. Fortunately, he didn't lean toward her too often.

"How long a drive is it to the Cotswolds?" she asked the driver.

"Ninety minutes or so. Little less maybe depending on traffic."

She reached into her bag to see if she missed any calls while underground. Nothing. "Patience still hasn't checked in."

"Perhaps she's been too busy."

"That's what I'm hoping." Too busy working out her problems with Stuart. "Do you know I still haven't told her about John Allen?"

"That could be for the best, since you haven't seen the painting yet. After you have met with Monsieur Allen, you will be able to give her much more information."

Like whether the collector would be willing to sell. "Do you think his position will change once he hears the painting's history?"

"It could. Or it could sway him the other way. Knowing the painting is attached to a world-renowned silver dynasty makes it—"

"Worth more, I know."

"Notoriety often does. Regardless, I'm sure no matter what the outcome of our meeting, Stuart Duchenko will spare no effort in trying to get his aunt's portrait returned."

"You are?"

"I know if it was something I wanted badly, I'd be relentless," he replied. The promise in his voice turned her insides upside down.

* * *

The English countryside was even more beautiful than the photos she saw online. Piper couldn't stop snapping pictures of the rolling green landscape.

"We have beautiful countryside in France as well," Frederic said, when she commented on a passing sheep farm.

"Yes, but that's French countryside. This is England," Piper countered. Spying a flock of grazing sheep, she took another photo.

"So?"

He almost sounded pouty. "You make it sound like it's a competition."

"It's always a competition when England is concerned."

"Well, at least it's easier to read the roadside signs here," she replied. Competition indeed. Both countries were better than any place she'd been before.

"Is there a place you can pull over so I can get a really good shot?" she asked the driver.

"The dozen or so you have already taken are not enough?" Frederic asked.

"I've got one more I want to take." And a moving car wouldn't do the subject justice.

"Will the shoulder ahead do?" He pointed to a particularly beautiful piece of scenery. A large checkerboard field in shades of green sprawled from the road to the horizon.

"Perfect."

The car slowed to a stop. "You have to get out, too," Piper told Frederic when he opened the door.

"Why?"

"Because I want you in the picture, that's why."

"A photograph of me standing on the side of the road."

"Actually, standing in front of that tree," she replied, pointing to a shrub-like tree a football field away.

From behind his sunglasses, Frederic was focusing in on her in his concentrated way. She tried to figure out his thoughts based on the rest of his expression, but it was impossible.

"Please?" she said, "I didn't think to take photos yesterday." Leaving her with zero visual evidence the magic day even happened. "I don't want to forget again this weekend." And be left with nothing.

"Only for you would I do this," he said.

"Thank you. Go stand by the tree and I'll be as quick as possible. Watch your step!" she added when he stepped down into a gulley.

"You're supposed to warn a person before they stumble," he said. Piper grinned. Hard to take the admonition seriously when he was grinning, too.

Not wanting to push her luck too much, she snapped three pictures in rapid succession. Her only regret was in forgetting to ask him to take off his sunglasses. She would have liked a picture with his eyes showing.

Maybe another time. "All done," she called to him. "You can get back into the car."

"Not yet. Gregory," he called to the driver, "Will you take mademoiselle's phone?"

"Yes, sir."

"You made us stop to take these photos. It is only fair you pose as well."

"Oh, no." Piper shook her head. "I hate having my picture taken."

"Gregory…"

The driver held out his hand expectantly.

"Watch out for the dip," Frederic said.

"Fine." Would be nice to have a photograph of her and Frederic for a memory. Giving her hair a quick fluff with her fingers, she stepped into the field.

Frederic met her under the tree. "Stand right here," he told her. Piper did as she was told, figuring they would pose side by side. Therefore she was caught off guard when Frederic moved behind her and wrapped his arms around her waist. "Smile for the camera," he murmured before pressing his cheek to Piper's temple.

"Got it," Gregory called.

Piper went to step forward, only to find herself held tight against Frederic's torso.

"Hold on," he said.

Keeping one arm around her waist, he caught her chin with the other, turned her head sideways and kissed her. Hard and thorough. "Now we can go."

Piper nearly forgot how to breathe. "What happened to no pressure?"

"No pressure, yes. I never said I wouldn't try to convince you, though, did I?" He held out a hand. "Shall we? Gregory is waiting."

"This is the inn John Allen recommended," Frederic said.

"It certainly is something," Piper replied.

It was a quintessential romantic country inn. A crooked building made of stone and quirky angles that sat at the top of the main street, while the rest of the village spread below. The whole thing was a postcard come to life. Thatched-roof buildings surrounded by rolling green hills and woodland. A local farmer driving his sheep down the road was all it needed to complete the picture.

It looked like the kind of place lovers went to hide. Precisely the kind of place a man would take a woman like Piper.

Why that thought left Frederic antsy, he wasn't sure.

The proprietress, a Mrs. Lester, met them at the front door. "You must be the people who called last night." She smiled widely. "You are lucky. We don't usually have rooms this time of year, but we had a family cancel at the last minute, leaving us with two rooms open."

He almost chuckled at Piper's relieved breath.

While Piper went in search of a Wi-Fi signal so she could contact her sister, Frederic made arrangements with Gregory for the next day, then went upstairs to lie down. His head ached. He was not used to traveling outside Paris anymore. Navigating unfamiliar locations and crowds took extra concentration. Especially Saint Pancras station, where he had the additional strain of translating signage.

He'd been pushing himself harder than usual the past couple days. Piper was having such a good time; he wasn't about to spoil her happiness by asking that they slow down. Besides, the truth was, he didn't want to slow down, either. He was having a good time, too. No knowing how many more days like these he would have.

He was breaking his own rule about taking things day by day. Something about Piper made him reflective.

As his head sank against the pillows, he turned his focus to a more pleasant thought: the kiss he stole earlier. He'd been craving a second kiss since their first one ended, and after three hours of forced proximity—where her vanilla scent surrounded him like a cloud—he could no longer wait. She tasted as sweet as he remembered. There was a delicious innocence to her kisses. Then, there was an innocence to her, too. As rocky as her childhood was, she still saw beauty in the world. She was the type of woman for whom fairy tales could exist. Look at how she was with her sister, going so far as to email Stuart Duchenko to salvage the sister's romance. She no doubt thought this portrait she was chasing represented a wonderfully tragic grand passion. It was infectious, this spirit of hers. Why else would he stand stupidly under a tree on the side of an English highway?

It was also why he made sure she understood from the start that whatever was between them would be a very finite fairy tale that would end when she returned to America.

Until then, though, he would show her a romantic time. And while he would not pressure her into his bed—he would never pressure any woman—he would do his best to convince her that his bed was where she wanted to be.

He must have fallen asleep, because the next thing he knew there was a soft knock on the door.

"I'm sorry," Piper said when he opened it. "Were you sleeping?"

"Dozing. Happens when I rest my eyes." He ran a finger through his hair, tugging the roots to clear the cobwebs. "Did you reach your sister?"

"I did. We had a good talk. I'm actually very hopeful for her and Stuart."

"That's good." He stepped aside to let her come in, only for her to start and stop. The way she toyed with the neckline of her jersey suggested she wasn't entirely sure what she wanted to do. Her hesitancy fit with all the other innocent facets of her personality.

It was utterly charming.

"I thought I'd take a walk through the village. See if any of those eight buildings was a gift shop. I was going to ask if you wanted to join me, but if you're not feeling well…"

"My eyes are tired is all," he replied.

"Do you want to rest?"

Hardly. "If I stayed behind every time my eyes weren't one hundred percent, I would never leave my house." And he would not be that person in a million years. "I would love to walk the village with you."

"You believe in pushing yourself, don't you?" she asked when they were downstairs. "I mean, you're on the go all the time."

"I don't believe in holding others back." An understatement if ever he made one. "And I believe in making the most of every moment."

"We've certainly crammed a lot of stuff into the past couple days, that's for certain."

He leaned close and said in a voice only she could hear, "The weekend is still young. Who knows what interesting activities we will discover." He didn't need peripheral vision to know he'd made her blush. So adorable.

Based on the village center, Frederic guessed this was not one of the Cotswold villages that catered to weekend travelers. They found a wine shop, a real estate business and a law firm. The only shop was an apothecary, where Piper bought a handful of postcards and two bottles of English lavender bath salts.

"What do you think?" she asked as she held the bottle under his nose. "Will it make a nice souvenir?"

"Very nice." Although her own scent was much nicer.

They contented themselves with walking the sidewalks after that. Piper was enchanted with the houses and hidden walkways. "I feel we walked onto a Hollywood set," she said, stopping to smell a hedge of blackberries. "If I were going to make a movie about an English country village, this is what it would look like."

Frederic had to admit, the gardens and brambles were beautiful. He liked the quiet. Moreover, he liked the comfortable silence the two of them shared. He noticed the other day that there wasn't a pressure to fill the space with noise the way there was with some of the women he spent time with. He was able to focus on navigating the uneven sidewalks without distraction. Well, almost without distraction, he thought, as his companion stopped to admire another garden. While he had been resting earlier, she pulled her hair into a ponytail. He liked when she wore her hair back; he could see her features better.

Because he could, he curled a stray hair behind her ear. She immediately ducked her head. "I don't know about you, but I'm getting hungry. I haven't eaten since the train," she said. Did she know her fingers were retracing the path he just made? "The man at the store told me there's a pub about a half mile to the north. The Hen & Chick or something like that. Should we try it out?"

"I don't think we have much choice. There seems to be an equal number of inns and restaurants."

"True," she said, smiling. "Considering how nice the rest of the town is, I don't see how the pub could be bad. And you did say to take things as they come…"

The subtext of her comment sent a thrill through him. "Good to see you're getting into the spirit."

"As far as dinner is concerned, anyway." She

ducked her head again, but he caught the tiny smile she was trying to hide nonetheless.

"Dinner's always a good start," he told her.

They started walking again. "I wonder what the chances are that this place has a traditional pub menu. I've always wanted to try steak and kidney pie. And steamed pudding. Like spotted dick or treacle."

Frederic had to laugh at her enthusiasm over her potential menu. "I'm beginning to understand why you became a chef. You clearly love food."

"Good food," she corrected. "I'll try anything once, but to be honest, some of the froufrou stuff I can do without."

"Froufrou?" He didn't understand.

"Overly fancy. I'm not a fan of when chefs try too hard with food. I mean, don't get me wrong. I'm all for mixing things up, but sometimes a steak is best when you leave it a plain old steak." She let out a soft laugh. "Guess that explains why Chef Despelteau hates me. He's the king of froufrou."

"I'm sure you're exaggerating, and he doesn't *hate* you."

"Don't be so sure. I know you think he's pushing me to be better, but I think he just doesn't groove on the way I cook. Hasn't since day one."

They were passing under an oak tree. She reached up and plucked one of the leaves. "You know, the other day when you found me crying in the kitchen, I was thinking of quitting," she told him.

"Really?" He knew she was upset, but thought she simply had a bad day. If she had quit, they wouldn't be walking this sidewalk. "What made you change your mind?"

"We worked too hard to get me to Paris. It'd be wrong not to see things through."

We. Meaning her sister and her. Frederic wasn't sure why, but talk of her sister and culinary school together unsettled him. There was an element of obligation to the way she talked about the combination that he didn't like.

"Surely if you are unhappy, your sister would

not want you to continue." At least not the sister she'd described to him. "She'd want you to be happy."

"Oh, she does," Piper replied. "She would tell me to come home in a second, but like I said, quitting doesn't feel right.

"Besides," she added, "I'm not unhappy. Not right now, anyway."

"I'll take that as a compliment." His satisfaction almost outweighed the uneasiness he was feeling on her behalf. "So you finish your coursework. What then? What will you do when you go back to Boston?"

"Get a job at one of the local restaurants and work my way up the chain," she said. "Isn't that what one does with a culinary certificate?"

Yes, but one usually sounded more enthusiastic about the prospect. Then again, most students enjoyed school as well. This was one of those times when he wished he could walk and focus on his companion at the same time. To be able to see what she was thinking.

"You could open your own restaurant. Café du Piper."

She laughed. "Someday, maybe. A little bistro where I could design my own menu. Patience and I used to talk about my doing that."

Again, Patience. The woman was beginning to bother him, she was so ubiquitous. "Are all your dreams tied to your sister?" he asked, sharply.

"No." But her voice was too defensive to be convincing. "I have plenty of my own dreams."

"Like what?" Suddenly, very interested in hearing what she wanted, Frederic stopped walking and positioned himself so he could look her in the eye. "If you could do anything you wanted, what would it be?"

"Cooking, of course."

"Is that all? Just cooking? Tell me, what is Piper's passion?"

He was glad he stopped if for no other reason than he was gifted with the sight of her lashes sweeping downward like a thick black curtain. "You'll think it's silly."

"No, I won't." There was nothing about her he'd ever find silly. "I'd truly like to know."

"All right, but I'll warn you, it's not all that fancy."

"No one said it had to be."

She took a deep breath. "If I could do anything in the world, I would spend my time cooking wonderful meals for the people who matter to me. Food was there for me when I needed a friend. I would like to give people the same gift.

"Told you it was silly," she said, turning her head.

"Not silly at all. It's a lovely sentiment." One that fit her perfectly. How lucky those people would be.

Leaning close, he kissed her cheek. "I hope you get your dream," he whispered.

Don't let it die for your sister's sake, he added silently.

The pub was called the Hen & Rooster, and while the plaque next to the front door said it was established in 1666, Piper was pretty sure it had been modernized many times. The blast of comfortable, clean-smelling air that greeted them upon entering was her clue.

Aesthetically, the inside looked exactly like a seventeenth-century tavern. So much so, in fact, that Piper almost expected the bartender to be wearing period clothing and a leather apron. The floors were slanted. The walls were uneven. As they were walking into the dining room, Frederic clipped the top of his head.

"Must not have had too many people taller than six foot," she teased.

"More like five. There should be a sign warning people. Or padding on the cross beams."

"Poor baby. Does this help?" She massaged the top of his head, where he had tapped the beam.

"Much better," he replied. She couldn't see his eyes for the sunglasses, but she could feel their stare on her skin nonetheless. Felt as if he was concentrating all his attention on her face. Her mouth, to be precise. Taking her hand in his, he brought it to his lips. "Thank you."

She slipped her hand free and fought the urge to run it nervously across the back of her neck. Amazing how the air between them shifted so quickly, easy one moment, humming with awareness the next.

Of course, the fact that he'd kissed her twice in ten minutes probably helped that cause along.

Other than a pair of men at the bar, the restaurant was empty. That didn't stop the hostess from placing them at a table in the corner near an unused fireplace. Intimate and romantic. What a surprise. Maybe there was a competition between France and England, after all. To see which one could make her fall under Frederic's spell the fastest.

She could have told them they needn't work so hard. Frederic was doing fine without their help. Desperate for a distraction, she studied the single-sheet menu the hostess handed her.

"Do they have your pie?" Frederic asked.

"Afraid not. Looks like the chef prefers more continental than traditional British. Unless quinoa is an English staple I didn't know about."

"I'm sorry."

"Me too," she said, giving an exaggerated sigh. More to best him in the dramatics department than anything. "I'll simply have to make do with roasted guinea fowl."

"Poor baby." Just like that, the mood went back to being easy. If only they'd struck up a friendship earlier in her employment. The year could have been so much nicer. In the back of her mind, she sent up a silent thank-you to Ana. Without her portrait, they would still be virtual strangers.

"Good evening. Can I take your order?" The bartender appeared at their table with a pad in his hand. Piper gave her order.

"The same, along with a bottle of sauvignon blanc," Frederic said when she was finished.

"Did you even look at the menu?" She saw him fingering the paper, but the sheet never actually left his plate.

"I trust your judgment. Plus, I left my magnifying glass in my overnight bag."

"Ahh, the truth comes out. Now it's my turn to hope you aren't disappointed."

"I haven't been so far."

A flutter danced through her. *Better be careful.* She already liked him more than she should.

Now that they were seated, he'd removed his sunglasses, giving her the chance to study him straight-on. What she saw left her feeling guilty. There were lines around his eyes and mouth. The kind that came with fatigue. He was rubbing his thumb and middle finger across his eyebrows, massaging the skin underneath.

She waited while the bartender served the wine, then asked him, "Eyes still tired?"

"A little."

She had a feeling the two of them had different definitions of the term. "You didn't have to come with me, you know. I could have gone sightseeing on my own." Wouldn't have been as enjoyable, but she would have endured.

"Absolutely not. I told you before, I am not going to sit in my room acting like an invalid because of a little eyestrain." The fierceness with which he spoke startled her. Way more than you'd expect for a simple suggestion.

He must have realized how sharp he sounded, too, because when he spoke again, his voice was softer and more in control. "I thought we settled this back at the inn."

"We did. But then I started thinking about how tired you looked. I feel bad that I didn't think about your needs."

Apparently, she said something wrong, because he immediate stiffened. "My need is for you not to accommodate me," he said, glaring over his wineglass.

"I only meant…"

"I know what you meant." Again, he corrected his voice, clearly trying to cover whatever nerve she'd touched with her comment. "I'm sorry," he said. "I don't mean to be sharp. Let us say I have done my share of accommodating people's needs in the past and it wasn't pleasant."

Clearly. "Would it help if I told you I won't be one of those women?" It was the only thing she could imagine had happened. That a former girl-friend had been overly demanding.

"It wasn't a woman."

Who, then? Piper watched as he rolled the stem of his glass back and forth between his fingers. His eyes were focused on the contents, but she had a feeling he wasn't really looking at the wine. Rather he was debating what kind of answer to give.

She wasn't sure why, but she expected some kind of clever deflection. Thus it surprised her when he said, "The problem with accommodating is that it is very easy for a person to turn someone else into their servant."

A harsh way of thinking. Whoever this person was must have really been demanding. "All I said was I could have gone to the drugstore alone. It's not like I offered to cut your meat or anything.

Although technically you could order me to do that since I am your servant."

That should have earned a laugh, but it didn't. Frederic simply went back to rotating his wineglass. His features had grown stormy; in the dim light, his eyes were like thunderclouds.

"My mother did everything for my father," he said.

"Some women are traditional that way." Even as she spoke, however, the words sounded flat.

"This had nothing to do with traditional. My father was incapable of doing anything without help. He needed my mother constantly. She had no life of her own. Everything revolved around him."

"You don't have to explain." She hoped he would—there was so much she wanted to know about him—but from his sudden hoarseness she could tell the subject was a painful one.

"What about all the things she did with you? You said the other day she exposed you to art..."

"I said she made sure I was exposed. The nanny

would take me, and when I came home, she and I would talk about what I saw." He looked down at his wine again. "To be fair, if she had a choice she would have taken me herself."

Piper knew all about not having choices. "Why was he so…" She wanted to say *selfish*, but it didn't seem her place.

"He was blind."

Piper blinked. "How?" It explained a lot.

"Retinitis pigmentosa is hereditary."

And Frederic, as the lucky heir, was doing his best to handle the disease differently than his father, was that it? Was that why he flew off the handle at what was a minor gesture of kindness? "I'm—" With a shake of her head, she cut the apology off. No way Frederic would want to hear her tell him she was sorry. Not now. So she said nothing.

"Let's talk about something else," Frederic said, breaking her thoughts. "I don't want to spoil the evening being maudlin. Tell me what you think about the wine."

Not wanting to spoil the evening either, Piper complied.

CHAPTER SEVEN

FREDERIC LISTENED AS Piper talked about how
she could never tell the difference between an
oak sauvignon blanc and a dry sauvignon blanc.
"You'd think I could, being a cook and all, but
wine is a whole different science," she said.

For the second time this week, he appreciated
how she knew when not to push. Perhaps because
of her own touchy childhood subjects, she understood when a conversation stepped too close to a
nerve. Whatever the reason, he was grateful she
decided to let the news about his father's blindness go by without comment.

Why he brought up the subject in the first place
was beyond him. He certainly didn't intend to.
His childhood was something he *never* discussed.
Sharing the past—sharing anything personal—

implied intimacy, which could lead a person to believe the relationship had a future. The last thing he wanted to do was mislead someone like Piper.

But then, he thought about all the secrets she'd shared about her childhood, and he started to feel as if he owed her some measure of equality. A secret for a secret. And so he shared his.

Now he wished he hadn't, because the memory was alive in his head. His father's voice, broken and slurred, the ice in his tumbler rattling. *I need you. I can't do it on my own.* "It" being so many things. Generations of being waited on by servants left their mark. His father had been left incapable of doing for himself. As a result, his neediness knew no bounds.

Frederic, on the other hand… He might have inherited his father's fortune, but his life taught him how not to need. And so he forced the conversation back to superficial, happy conversation, and Piper, bless her heart, played along.

It helped that dinner turned out to be delicious.

"See?" he said, setting his fork down. "I was right to trust your judgment. I enjoyed my fowl."

"It wasn't bad," she replied. "Though I would have cut back on the thyme."

"Would that make the dish thyme-less?"

The tinkle of her laugh left him wanting to hear more. It was disturbing how easy he found her company. She was fun, she was smart. And, her kisses aroused him in a way he hadn't felt since his teenage years.

A hollow feeling started to spread behind his breastbone, causing him to squeeze his hand into a fist. Ninety-nine days out of one hundred, he accepted his future without complaint. Every so often, however, he would feel the ache for what he would miss. Unless he decided to be as self-ish as his father...

I need you, Patrice. His father's constant mantra.

Frederic would not need. Would never need.

He could, however, *want*, and at the moment,

he wanted the woman seated across from him very much.

Piper gave a soft cough. She knew he was studying her. "I was cursing the poor lighting," he said. "I want to be able to see you better." Her cheeks were no doubt turning as crimson as the roses they passed on their walk. Would the color spread to other parts of her body?

He reached across the table for her hand, feeling a victorious thrill when she met him halfway. "Do you still want your pudding?" he asked, playing with her fingers.

"I didn't see it listed on the menu."

"What a shame. I would hate for you to miss out on dessert."

"I'm sure I'll find something that will tempt me." She leaned closer and added, "On the menu."

The little minx. Two could play that game. "You should know," he said, leaning as well, "that when we're finished here, I plan to kiss you senseless. Then I'm going to kiss you again."

He might not be able to see her face clearly in

the shadows, but he definitely heard her breathing quicken.

"Now that I think about it," she said, "I don't have to have the cheesecake."

"Good." Not bothering to signal for the bill, he took out his wallet and tossed down a stack of notes thick enough to cover ten dinners and grabbed her hand. "Let's go."

Amazingly, he made it the entire walk back without pulling her into his arms. Safety first, he reasoned. Kissing her would obliterate his concentration.

He also took masochistic pleasure in pushing the anticipation to its peak. He tortured himself by holding only her hand on the walk, and when they climbed the stairs to their rooms, he walked a step behind so that her that her vanilla scent filled his nostrils.

When they reached the top of the staircase, he finally broke and put his hands on her waist. From the trembling beneath his fingers, he knew he was not the only one who had been tortured.

"I believe I promised you something," he said, turning her around.

Cupping her cheeks, Frederic focused all his attention on her lips. Last night was but an appetizer. Tonight, he would take his time. Savor. He kissed one corner of her mouth, then the other. Her quickened breath was his reward. When he finally lowered his mouth to hers, she let out a whimper. Relief.

"My room or yours?" he whispered when they broke to breathe.

"Doesn't matter."

She was right. It didn't. He reached for a door.

"There you are. I've been knocking on your door for ten minutes."

Piper looked up from the French press she'd been timing. Frederic stood barefoot in the dining room doorway, his shirt untucked and buttoned incorrectly. He looked the picture of a man who had just rolled out of bed. Which, of course, he had. Piper knew because up until an hour ago, she'd been in bed with him.

Thinking about what they did there made her flush.

"Mrs. Lester and I were talking about break-fast recipes," she replied, her voice overly bright. Could she sound any more like she was try-ing to be in control? "I gave her the recipe for huevos rancheros and she's going to give me hers for bangers and mash."

"The least I can do after all your help," Mrs. Lester replied. The innkeeper swiped back an errant red curl. "Guests aren't supposed to be allowed in the kitchen, but hard to say no to a real chef."

"I might have done a little of the prep work while we were talking," Piper added, sheepishly. She needed something to burn off her nervous energy. Speaking of…she checked to see if the grounds had brewed long enough. "Would you like some coffee?"

"I'm surprised you're awake so early," Frederic

said. Leaning forward, he added in a voice only she could hear, "I wasn't expecting to find your side of the bed empty."

Piper shivered as his voice tickled her ear. "You were asleep," she told him. "I didn't want to wake you."

And okay, maybe she might have wanted to avoid any potential morning-after awkwardness. Last night had been amazing, with a capital *A*, but she knew as well as anyone that night and morning were two vastly different times of day, and what seemed like a good idea after a couple glasses of wine might look like a disaster in the daylight. She was afraid to face the regret in Frederic's eyes.

It wasn't regret she was seeing right now, however. The expression looking down on her was as predatory as ever. "My ego is hurt," he said. "Usually when I am with a woman, it's the other way around. I must be losing my touch."

No, he definitely wasn't losing that. Piper's insides melted from simply thinking about the things his hands could do. She looked over her shoulder to see if Mrs. Lester had heard. The innkeeper had her head in the oven, checking on pans of bread dough.

"I'm sorry. I started thinking about this morning's meeting and couldn't fall back asleep." It wasn't a complete lie. She did think about the meeting in passing. "I decided to come down here for a cup of coffee, and that's when I ran into Mrs. Lester."

"Who put you to work making your huevos ranchos. Come back to bed."

"Huevos *rancheros*," she corrected automatically, "and I wasn't just giving her the recipe. I was making breakfast potatoes."

"Come back to bed." His lips moved to her ear again despite Mrs. Lester being a room away. "I want to show you what you missed by leaving early."

Piper's knees buckled. "Is—is it all right if we take the coffee upstairs?" she asked Mrs. Lester.

"Sure thing," Mrs. Lester replied. "Leave the

press in your room, and I'll have the cleaning girl bring it down. Thank you, too, for your help this morning. First time I ever have had a guest who made breakfast potatoes better than me."

"That's sweet of you to say. We'll be back down—" Frederic was pushing her toward the stairwell. "You didn't let me finish," she said to him.

"I don't care," he replied. "Do you have any idea how many downstairs rooms I looked in before I found you?"

"There are only three."

"Three too many. Now, back to our room with you, young lady. The door is unlocked."

Our room. The words gave Piper as big a thrill as Frederic's intentions. With his hands holding her waist, Piper climbed the stairs.

A couple hours later, they were back in the dining room, showered and ready for the day.

Mrs. Lester greeted them with a knowing smile that had Piper blushing again. "Sit anywhere you'd like. You're the last ones for the day.

"By the way," she added, "Your driver arrived while you were upstairs." Gregory sat at a corner table reading the paper. He too gave them a smile and a nod.

"The whole room knows what we were doing," she whispered to Frederic.

"You mean Gregory, and I don't think he's surprised. If anything, he is jealous. I know I would be in his shoes."

All it took was a trace of his finger running down her forearm and Piper melted again.

"Do you do this often?" she asked him.

"Steal away to England with a beautiful woman?" When she didn't take the bait, he grew more serious. "My bedpost doesn't have too many notches, if that is what you're asking."

That was exactly what she was asking. Now that he had answered, Piper realized that he rarely stayed away all night. He had guests in his house even less. Off the top of her head, she remembered one, possibly two, and they had both gone home before breakfast.

"I'm glad." Based on the way his eyes widened, her honesty surprised him. "No woman wants to think she is one in a long line." Knowing there were but a few women made her less mundane, to steal one of Chef Despelteau's words. More in keeping with what Frederic meant to her.

Mrs. Lester appeared, pot of coffee in hand, to end the conversation. "Piper tells me you're meetin' with John Allen this morning. About a painting."

"We are," Frederic replied. "Do you know him?"

"A bit. Comes in here for tea now and again. A queer little fella, he is—I don't mean that in the politically insensitive way or nothing. He's just quirky."

"Quirky, how?" Piper asked. They were heading to the man's house. If he was a crazy person, she'd like to know.

"Little things really. Like he always insists on bringing his own pastries when he comes here. Richest man in town and he won't pay for a bloody scone, but then leaves a one hundred and fifty percent tip."

"Sounds like he's very particular," Frederic said over his coffee cup.

"*Particular* is a good word for it. I've got one last basket of breads. Do you folks want it?"

"Yes, please," Piper replied. Once Mrs. Lester was out of earshot, she looked back in Frederic's direction. "Is *particular* good or bad, do you think?" It sounded suspiciously like Bernard's selectivity, if you asked her.

The Frenchman shrugged. "Hard to say. Art collectors are a bit like snowflakes. No two are the same."

"Maybe I'll get lucky, and Ana's story will break his heart to the point he wants her to have the painting."

"Or your friend Stuart will write enough zeroes that he can't refuse."

"He's not my friend—he's Ana's great-nephew. And hopefully Patience's—"

"Friend?" he finished with a smirk to rival Mrs.

Lester's. He dragged the word out, long and with plenty of subtext.

"When you say it that way, Stuart is definitely not my friend." Piper reached for her coffee. She wasn't forgetting that *friend* was also how he described their relationship.

His lips were wet with coffee as he smiled from across the table. "I'm glad. I don't like sharing."

He didn't like to share and he didn't like to think about tomorrow. Kind of put her in limbo, didn't it?

John Allen's house was at the end of a long road tucked between two giant lavender fields. With nothing marking the turn, they drove past the place twice before locating the winding dirt road. Considering Allen was supposed to be a wealthy patron of the arts, Piper had been expecting someplace more upscale and artsy, or at the very least, someplace large, not this crooked cottage with a thatched roof. But then, maybe this was what passed for artsy and upscale out here. They were in the middle of nowhere. She looked for a car, but the only item with wheels was a bicycle propped by the garden shed.

"Are you sure we have the right address?" she asked Gregory.

"GPS says we do."

"Perhaps he is trying to discourage thieves," Frederic said.

That was one theory. Stepping out of the car, she was greeted by the smell of flowers and freshly tilled dirt.

"It appears Monsieur Allen does not believe in landscaping," Frederic remarked as he joined her. He had a point. Time and rain had cut deep ruts into the dirt driveway, turning the already-rough surface into a bumpy hazard. There were primroses that lined the walk leading to the door, and a container of annuals, but other than that, the outside of the cottage was bare. "Maybe he figures the lavender fields were enough."

"Perhaps." Frederic took a deep breath. "The aroma certainly is pervasive."

"The better to hide bodies. A joke," she said when he turned with a frown. She slipped her hand into his, stealing comfort from his grip. "I'm glad you are here."

Something she couldn't read flickered across his face. "Thank you," he said, squeezing her fingers. He looked about to say more when the cottage door flew open.

"Helloo!" the newcomer greeted. "You must be Piper. It's good to see you. I was worried you'd gone and got yourself lost." With his thick accent, the last word sounded more like "loost." "And you brought a friend. Hullo." He smiled widely in Frederic's direction.

Mrs. Lester's description suddenly made sense. Dressed from head to toe in white linen, John Allen looked like a miniature version of a 1920s English gentleman. The crown of his silver head barely reached Piper's nose. How on earth could Bernard not remember meeting him?

Piper introduced them, and he shook Frederic's hand enthusiastically. "Call me John, please. Both of you."

"Thank you for meeting with us," Piper said.

"Well, I must admit you have me curious. I had no idea my impulse purchase had such notoriety."

Frederic caught her attention and pointed a finger upward, letting her know where the price would be heading.

Unlike the outside, which looked ignored, the inside was a modern showplace. John had knocked down several walls to open one large room with vaulted ceilings. There was a kitchen that could rival Frederic's. Piper was half tempted to chuck looking at art so she could explore the appliances. Out of the corner of her eye, she saw Frederic doing his best to take in details.

Their host noticed as well. "Bought the place on the cheap at auction a few years ago, I did," he replied when Frederic complimented him. "Had to completely gut the place, though. Didn't hold up in the wet and got a bad case of rot. Place is climate-controlled now. Wouldn't hang the canvases until it was installed."

"Sound thinking," said Frederic.

"I thought so. Seemed daft to spend a fortune and not see to it properly. The main collection is on the back wall."

"How many pieces do you have?" Piper asked.

"Right now? Fifteen. A couple of the larger works are on loan in New York. Haven't got the space here."

She could see why. The large back wall had half a dozen paintings already. Frederic was squinting at a watercolor of a woman tilling a garden. "Bergdahl?" he asked.

"Good eye, Professor. Bought it from a gallery in New York around twenty years ago."

"His pieces seldom come on the market now."

"I heard a rumor one of his seascapes might be going up for sale next month. I've already let my man know I'm interested. Ana's back here, in my dining room. Help yourself to tea and scones, by the way. I baked them myself."

Piper tugged on Frederic's sleeve. "I hate to sound tacky, but how much would you pay for that painting? It was barely the size of a piece of copy paper."

"Trust me, you do not want to know."

John was waiting in the dining room doorway. "And here she is. *Ana Reclining*."

"Wow" was all Piper could say. Hard to believe the woman reclining on the settee was the same little old woman who popped in to say hello during one of their video chats.

"Beautiful, isn't she?" John said.

"Breathtaking."

"I fell in love the moment I saw her. I love how he made her skin so luminous-looking. And her lips. The way he caught them in mid sigh? Doesn't she look like a woman who'd just been—"

"Right," Piper said. This was her sister's elderly boss they were talking about. Some images were best left to the imagination.

Unfortunately, John was right. The painting

dripped with sensuality. It wasn't the sexiness that caught your attention, though. At least not as far as Piper was concerned. It was Ana's expression. She was looking at the artist with nothing short of adoration. They weren't looking at a seventeen-year-old girl draped naked across a sofa. They were looking at a woman in love. Piper wondered if that wasn't the reason Theodore Duchenko wanted all the paintings destroyed.

She tried to imagine how it would feel, to be that deeply in love and have it ripped away from you.

"Are you all right?" John asked.

"Fine. I was thinking about poor Ana Duchenko is all. She's going to be so happy to know this painting survived." She reached into her bag for her cell phone. "You said I could take a few photographs?"

"Yes, yes. Be my guest. Just make sure the flash is off, if you don't mind. I don't want the colors to fade."

"Thank you." Whether he sold Stuart the painting or not, Ana needed to see proof her love for Nigel still existed on canvas.

While she clicked away, John maneuvered his way around the dining room table to pour tea. Frederic, meanwhile, had moved to the opposite of the room to study the painting. Piper caught the telltale movement of his head that said he was looking at it in sections.

"You said on the phone, you were trying to locate the painting for the real Ana?" John handed her a teacup, then offered one to Frederic.

"Ana Duchenko," Piper replied. She proceeded to tell him the story. As the details poured out, she realized she was destroying any chance Stuart had at buying the painting cheaply, but that didn't matter. It was more important John Allen understand that the painting was more than "notorious."

"Fascinating," John said. "So as far as you know, this is the only painting left that Nigel Rougeau painted."

"Unless someone has one hidden in their basement, yes." Frederic gave a soft cough, a warning that she ignored. "Nigel died shortly after Ana went back to the States."

John gave an odd sigh. "Such a tragic story. I knew that painting had to be a work of love the first time I saw it. You can see the emotion in her eyes."

So he did understand. "You know, Ana never married."

"She didn't?"

Piper shook her head. She felt as if she were gossiping about some old Hollywood romance the way her host was hanging on every word. "She lives in Boston with her cat, Nigel."

"The cat is named Nigel?" John clutched his chest. "I think I might cry."

"So you can see why her nephew wants to buy the painting. He wants to return the portrait to her while she's still alive."

"That's such an amazing story," John said. "To think, poor Nigel, robbed of his potential greatness. Can you imagine what he could have achieved if Theodore Duchenko hadn't destroyed his work?" He looked to Frederic, as if waiting for confirmation.

"A genuine loss," Frederic replied.

"Not to mention a great inspiration," Piper added. She snapped a few more pictures to be safe. She'd already made a mental note to send Nigel's sister a copy as well. "I think Ana really was his muse."

"I think so, too. I see why her nephew wanted to track the work down."

"The question is…" For the first time since they'd sat down, Frederic addressed the elephant in the room. "Would you be willing to sell her?"

"Well…" John drew out the word for several beats. Never a good sign. "I'll be glad to talk with Mr. Duchenko, of course, but like I said, she is one of my favorite pieces. I love looking at her while I eat."

That was an image Piper could do without.

They spent another hour or so looking at the

rest of the collection, the older man thrilled to show his paintings to someone who "appreciated them." When they were finished, Piper once again urged him to consider selling *Ana Reclining*.

"I promise I'll think about it," he said. "I do have a soft spot for star-crossed lovers."

"Thank you." Looking at Ana's portrait one last time, she crossed her fingers that the painting would be heading to Boston soon.

"Mrs. Lester was right," she said when they were on the way to the car. "He is quirky."

"Quirky but savvy. His collection is amazing. The Bergdahl alone was worth the trip.

"Congratulations, by the way." With his arm around her shoulders, Frederic kissed her temple. "Your treasure hunt was a success."

Yeah, it was. Still, Piper frowned.

"Is something wrong?"

"I don't know. I thought I'd be more excited, but…"

"You're sad because your hunt is over. That is not unusual."

It was more than the end of the hunt. She was reminded all of a sudden that looking for Ana's painting was what kept Frederic in her orbit. Now that the search was over, would she be enough to make him stay around? Or would their affair be over when they returned to Paris?

She really stank at this taking-things-as-they-come stuff.

"These last couple days of adventure have spoiled me." In more ways than one.

"The day is not over. We can still have adventures."

"Like what?" she asked, as if she couldn't guess already.

Frederic stopped walking and stared at her with a focus Piper had never seen before. Part desire, part…confusion? Whatever the emotions behind his eyes, it set off a slow burn in the pit of her stomach.

"May I show you something?" he asked, running his thumb across her lower lip.

"Of course," she replied. When he looked at her like that, he could show her anything.

CHAPTER EIGHT

IT HAD TO be the ugliest painting Piper had ever seen. Not depressing ugly like the painting in Bernard's gallery, but ugly-ugly. From what she could tell, the mural had been a group effort. Different sections reflected different styles. In the center of the mess, Saint Michael wrestled a fire-breathing dragon. At least the description said it was a dragon. Piper thought it looked more like a winged cow. The army of angels behind him was one giant block of white and gold, on which black lines had been painted to represent limbs while the villagers on the ground...she wasn't quite sure what the artist was thinking when he painted them. As for poor Saint Michael, he was rewarded with a protruding nose and lips so large he looked as if the dragon had slammed his face into a rock.

To her right, Frederic beamed at the work like a man looking at his child. "Saint Michael vanquishing evil," he said, reverence in his voice. "What do you think?"

"Umm, it's different."

"Have you ever seen anything so ugly? It's even worse than I remembered."

Oh, good. She was afraid she was going to have to pretend something way beyond her acting skills.

They were in the chamber by themselves, the abbey ruins not being one of the area's more popular attractions. Piper could see why. Ugly mural aside, there wasn't much else to see. Much of the monastery had fallen into ruin. Only the room they were in survived.

She turned back to the painting. "You wrote a paper on this piece?" After all the beautiful things he'd shown her the past couple of days, it was a bit of a letdown.

And yet Frederic seemed thoroughly enchanted. "Yes, I did."

"Why?" She had to be missing something. Maybe there was some historical connection she didn't understand.

Taking her hand, he led her closer. "Because I don't think this painting was ever about being good. The men who painted it had to know they didn't have talent. Or perhaps they thought they did. It doesn't matter. This painting is perfect because of its flaws. You see ugly, I see joy. Passion."

The passion was Frederic's. You could feel it radiating off him as he spoke. Like the day in the Place des Vosges, only ten times stronger.

"Of all the paintings I have seen in my life, this is one of my favorites. Because it is pure."

"When you put it that way." Piper's heart was suddenly too big for her chest. She felt so amazingly honored that he would share the piece with her. Wanting to thank him for the gift, but afraid he'd hear the emotion in her voice, she settled for a smile. "To think, all the other tourists will look and see a saint with swollen lips."

"Poor Saint Michael. He does look like he's had one too many collagen treatments, doesn't he?"

"I'm glad you got to see him again."

"I am, too."

They studied the mural in silence. Or rather, Frederic studied the painting while Piper studied him. From the moment this affair began, back in the kitchen in Paris really, she'd been haunted by a sense of surrealism, unable to believe they were together in the first place. Now this. She could feel herself starting to fall. If she hadn't already fallen, that is.

"Can I show you something else?" he asked.

"Here? At the abbey?" Frederic nodded before catching her hand in his again.

"It is outside," he told her.

Behind the monastery, the land spilled into a large grassy field dissected by boulders and a few errant black-eyed Susans. Still holding hands, they picked their way across the uneven ground until they reached the top of a large swell. From there they could look out over the entire abbey grounds. They were high enough that Piper could make out the shape of the old building in the ruined rock.

Frederic sat down, then tugged on her wrist so she would join him. They sat back on their elbows, legs stretched out in front of them.

"When I was studying the mural, I would take my lunch in this spot," he told her.

"It's beautiful." Taking out her phone, she snapped a picture. She was going to want to remember this day when she returned to Boston in a couple months.

She was going to want to remember a lot of things.

Off to their left, she spotted a roped-off section where the ground appeared dotted with markers. "Wonder what is going on other there?" she said, pointing.

"Archaeological research, no doubt. Before the abbey, this was a pagan ritual site."

"No way."

"It's the reason the abbey was built here in the first place. They would have painted Saint Michael as a way of discouraging rituals and protecting the land from evil."

"He does look scary. Wonder if it worked."

"You'll have to ask the pagans. From what I understand, there are some who come every solstice."

Kicking off her sandals, Piper wiggled her bare toes, enjoying the feel of the sun on her skin. The air was quiet but for the birds and buzzing bugs. Now that she thought about it, there was a kind of mystical feel to the air. Although she was certain it had more to do with her companion.

She turned and snapped a photo of him. His attention on the view, Frederic didn't notice.

When he was studying something very closely, his focus would grow intense, with all his energy directed at his target. It was more than simply trying to see; it was as if he was trying to see into whatever it was he was looking at. Piper had felt that intensity directed at her more than once. Each time, she'd melted under its strength.

This time she saw a sadness to his stare. She brushed the hair from his face to bring him back. "Trying to find a pagan?" she teased. Seeing the enthusiasm fading from his face had made her heart ache. "You're a million miles away."

"Sorry," he said, giving her a half a smile. "I don't know when I will be back here, so I was trying to memorize the view."

Piper was about to tell him that wasn't necessary because she'd taken pictures when she realized what he was really saying.

"I wasn't thinking," she said softly.

"I have read theories that if you stare at something long enough, the image will become ingrained in your memory. I don't know if blind people can see their memories or not, but in case they can…"

"Is that why you are always looking at the Eiffel Tower?" And at her?

"One of the reasons."

The full force of what lay in his future hit her. It was easy to forget with his matter-of-factness, but there would come a day when he couldn't see the sun or the grass. Not even his own hand. She couldn't imagine. A man who loved visual beauty as much as he did. Who saw beauty in ugly art.

"What are you going to do?" she asked him. "I mean, when…" A sob threatened, and she pushed it back along with the rest of her question.

"Carry on, of course. What else can I do?"

"Nothing, I suppose."

She watched as he plucked at the grass between them. Tugging blade after blade, only to discard each one atop a small pile of clippings. "Tell you what I won't do," he said. "I won't turn myself into a victim, making the whole world bow to my disability."

Like his father? That was what he meant, wasn't it? He did call his father needy last night.

"I asked him once," Frederic said, switching gears, "when I first learned I might have the disease, what it was like to be blind."

"What did he say?"

"He told me it was awful, and that I would find out for myself soon enough."

"That's it?" No reassurance, no advice? Surely the man wouldn't be so self-involved as to leave his son to face the unknown without some kind of support?

But then parents could be selfish. Hadn't her mother been more interested in everything other than Piper?

"Saying more would require him dealing with his own blindness. My father was more interested in wallowing. And in his cocktails," he added, swiping at the grass clippings. "Did you know I could make the perfect *soixante-quinze* when I was eight years old? That is gin and champagne, if you were wondering."

Piper wasn't. The little boy forced to make them was far more interesting. She wished she could tell him she understood what that was like, that she'd been in his shoes. Oddly enough, however, alcohol abuse wasn't one of her mother's many crimes.

"I can still picture him. Proving you can memorize an image," he added with a toneless laugh. "He had this giant easy chair where he would sit and listen to the stereo. All day long. Every day. He only left the house if my mother took him. I was so relieved when they decided to send me to boarding school, because it meant I wouldn't have to see him in that chair anymore."

Relieved, but guilty, too. Piper could hear the regret in his voice. He'd escaped to school, but his mother had stayed behind.

"I'm sorry," she said. "He must have been in a lot of pain."

"What he was, was a selfish bastard who never should have married my mother in the first place. He knew he was going blind. A real man wouldn't have asked her to stay."

No, he would have lived in the present and made no promises for tomorrow. A chill swept through Piper. "How do you know your mother didn't want to stay?" She already knew his answer from last night; Frederic believed his mother stayed out of guilt.

"How would she know that life would stop the moment my father lost his sight. If you're trying to defend him, you're wasting your time. I lived it. I watched day in and day out while she took care of him. Waited on him, walked with him. She cut his meat, for God's sake, while I..."

Stayed out of the way and made cocktails. No wonder his mother sent him away finally. Just imagining what it had been like for him made Piper's heart ache.

Frederic looked up. "Sometimes I wonder why they ever had a child."

Because once upon a time, they were in love and believed in the future. At least his mother had. Piper longed to tell him that it was okay. That it was okay for him to want more than a moment in the present.

You mean to want you. Tears burning the back of her throat, she rolled onto her side. "I'm glad your father was selfish," she told him. "Because if he hadn't been, we never would have met."

"Then he did something good after all."

The back of his hand caressed her cheekbone. Piper grabbed it and kissed his knuckles. It was her time to memorize for the future. "Thank you for showing me your ugly mural," she said.

"It's not my ugly mural. It belongs to Great Britain."

As far as she was concerned, the painting belonged to him, and she would be forever grateful that he chose her to share it with. Frederic would never know how special being here made her feel. She was beginning to understand the joy the monks must have felt when creating their art. Her heart was suddenly so full she feared it would burst.

She wanted to tell him. But how could she explain without sounding like a lovesick idiot that his sharing this part of himself—that these past few moments of vulnerability—meant everything to her?

There were words, three very huge words that summed up everything in her heart, but she wasn't ready to say them out loud. The feelings were too new, too fresh; now wasn't the time to say them. Piper wasn't sure there would ever be a time.

"I don't care who owns this place," she said. "There's still no place in England I would rather be."

Damn his sunglasses for blocking his eyes. She couldn't tell if he was happy or frightened by her admission. Halfway committed, there was nothing to do but keep going. "Or anyone else I'd rather be with."

"Piper, you know that I can't give you…I won't be selfish like my father."

"I know." But it broke her heart, too. He was telling her that he planned to live out his blindness alone because his father was a self-absorbed drunk, and he couldn't be more wrong. He could—should—have more. Arguing the point, though, would only break the moment. And in the end, he'd still believe the same way.

Better she go along. At least for now. "Hey…" Reaching for his sunglasses, she pulled them away so she could finally look him in the eye. "You're not blind yet. And I'm right here."

She watched as slowly the gray grew black with desire. "Here, and beautiful."

His palms were warm as they brushed the hair from her eyes. "I never want this picture to fade."

His kiss was slow and possessive. It wrapped around her soul, binding them together. Piper gladly gave herself over. Their surroundings disappeared. It was just them, the birds and the grass. When his hands grew bold, she clutched at his back. When they slipped beneath her shirt, she whimpered. And when the moment was over, and he lay heavy, his breath sounding in her ear, she had to bite back the emotions fighting to get out. Her heart belonged to him. Taking one day at a time had just become impossible.

And she was sunk.

* * *

Later that night, Frederic lay in bed staring at the ceiling. In the pitch-black bedroom, he couldn't see beyond shapes, but that did not matter. His mind was at the abbey. He was reliving the afternoon frame by frame so as to not forget a moment. *Thank you for showing me your ugly mural.*

What an amazing five days. To think, all these months there'd been a treasure living under his roof and he'd had no idea. Piper wasn't like other lovers he'd shared a bed with, and not simply because she was American and from a world different from his. The difference had nothing to do with sophistication or worldliness, although her guilelessness was amazingly erotic.

No, what made her different was the way everything felt magnified when he was with her. Bigger, brighter, stronger. *More.*

If only he'd discovered her gifts sooner. So much time wasted.

Well, he would not waste further. Between now

and when Piper returned to Boston, he would show her a time she'd never forget.

When Piper returned to Boston… The thought left a chill. He'd miss her. More than he thought possible. Somehow, over the past five days, she'd slipped under his skin to become someone special.

What was he supposed to do, though? Ask her to stay indefinitely? How fair was that?

No, better to give her a magical few weeks and then set her free. She would move on. Find a man who appreciated her, and he would have a wonderful memory to hold on to when the world grew dark.

Beside him, there was the rustle of sheets as Piper curled her body closer. Sliding one arm across his chest, she rested her head on his shoulder. Automatically, he began stroking her skin, seeking the contact that he could never seem to get enough of. "I thought you were asleep."

"Couldn't. Someone is thinking too loudly. Is everything all right?"

The gentle concern in her voice made his heart seize. For a brief moment, he let himself be wrapped up in her compassion. *If only*, he caught himself thinking.

"That wasn't thinking, that was my stomach," he said. "We missed dinner, you know."

"Whose fault is that?"

"Yours. For being irresistible." He kissed the teasing out of her voice, smiling at the tiny moan she made deep in her throat. "But now I am hungry."

"I can fix that," she whispered against his lips.

"Can you now?" In the back of his mind, he wondered if the hunger he felt for her could ever be completely satisfied. Like everything else, it was greater than he thought possible.

He reached for her, but to his disappointment, she slipped from his grasp. There was more rustling. Clothes. She was getting dressed.

"What are you doing?" he asked when she opened the door. Light from the hallway spilled through the crack into the room.

"Told you," she said. "I'm taking care of your hunger. Be right back."

"I know a better way," he called to her. But she'd already closed the door.

Alone, he went back to contemplating the dark ceiling. His eyes were unusually scratchy and tired tonight. Too much time in the sunlight. He had been overdoing things the past few days. Perhaps he should slow down. Or perhaps not. There would be plenty of time to slow down when he was alone.

He must have lost track of time, because before he realized, the door swung open.

"Voilà!" Piper announced. "Food."

Squinting, Frederic tried to see what Piper held in her hands. With the light behind her, however, all he could see was a hazy silhouette. "We have apples, candy bars and a package of something called McVitie's, which I think are cookies."

"How on earth did you find all this?"

"Mrs. Lester keeps a stash of snacks in the front room in case guests get hungry when the kitchen is closed. I found it when she asked me to restock the cabinet this morning."

"She asked you to restock *and* cook?" Even though she couldn't see him, Frederic grinned. "Should I be worried that Mrs. Lester hired you while I wasn't looking?"

A cellophane-wrapped package landed on the pillow near his head. "Shut up—I was doing her a favor. Can you switch on the nightstand lamp? My hands are full."

"Do you mind if we leave the lights off?" he asked her.

"Why? Are your eyes bothering you?"

Again, the concern in her voice gripped him with a warmth that made him want to hold her tight. "No," he said. "My eyes are fine." A small lie, not that it mattered. His eyes weren't the reason. There was an intimacy to the darkness he wasn't ready to give up.

Sliding out from beneath the covers, he crossed to the window and pulled back the wooden shutters. A beam of soft silver lit the floor by his feet.

"A picnic in the moonlight," Piper remarked as she joined him on the bed. "Romantic."

"I blame the company," he teased. "You inspire the romantic in me."

"You'd be the first." Her voice was soft, barely a whisper. Had there been street traffic or some other kind of outside noise, Frederic would have missed the comment altogether. Realizing he heard her, she quickly added a louder, "Sorry."

"Don't be." If it was up to him, she'd have romance every day. He cursed those idiots at school who were too blind to see her gifts. "Anyone who isn't inspired by you is a fool."

"Eat your snacks," she murmured. Frederic could practically hear the blush darkening her cheeks.

A comfortable silence settled over the room, punctuated only by the occasional sound of cellophane crinkling. This was nice, he thought. Comfortable. A man could become very attached to feeling this way if he wasn't careful. So attached he might not want to let go. Longing sprang to his chest, its strength catching him off guard. *You're going to be very hard to give up, aren't you, Piper?*

Piper's voice drifted from across the bed. "Penny for your thoughts?"

"I was thinking we should make the most out of the next couple months," he replied. "Make them unforgettable."

"I'd like that."

"Good. Why don't we start right now?" Rolling to his side, he kissed her into the pillow.

He woke to his face buried in a pillow and an empty bed. Vaguely, he remembered Piper saying something about cooking with Mrs. Lester. The older woman was definitely taking advantage of having another chef in the house. Looked as if he was going to have to go pry Piper away again. Yawning, he lifted his head.

No...

Something was wrong. While he could see, everything he looked at was hazy and faded, as though someone had wrapped the world with a thin gray film.

Frederic held up his hand. His trembling fingers were five muted shapes. Not even squinting could bring back the sharpness.

He willed himself to take a deep breath. No need to panic yet. His eyes could simply be over-tired. God knows, he'd pushed himself very hard the last couple days. Give his eyes a little more rest; that is what he should do. Sleep a little longer. He closed his eyes and focused on his breathing.

An hour later, however, nothing had changed. He was still staring into a haze.

Frederic's heart started to race. He wiped a hand over his face. *Do not jump to conclusions,* he reminded himself.

Making his way to the bathroom, he grabbed his shaving kit and dumped the contents on the vanity. He must have packed eye drops in case his eyes got tired. Slowly, he scanned the items on the counter. Which one was the eye drops? In his new blurry world, all the small bottles looked suspiciously alike. For all he knew, he could squirt his eyes with alcohol. Perhaps Piper...

No. He wasn't going to run to Piper, no matter how appealing the thought might be. The situation wasn't anything he hadn't struggled with before. Inhaling deeply, he looked again. The bottles were color-coordinated. Eye drops were in the green bottle. Where was the green bottle?

On the edge of his bathroom sink at home. He had used them right before they departed. Distracted by thoughts of Piper, he forgot to repack them.

No problem. He would simply go into the village and buy more.

Took some stumbling around the room—the room was foreign and he hadn't exactly been thinking of maintaining order when taking Piper to bed last night—but he finally got dressed. Then, with one hand on the wall, he made his way down the stairs.

His foot was barely on the landing when he nearly collided with a warm, familiar body.

"Whoops! You almost ended up wearing your coffee. Sorry about that." Piper's voice greeted him, warm and sweet. His first thought was to lean into her until the knot in his stomach went away. "I was going to leave the pot on the nightstand for when you woke up. Guess I was down here longer than I thought."

Her fingers touched his cheek. "I don't think I've ever seen you without a shave. I like the look. Very sexy." She stepped back. "Is everything all right?"

No, he wanted to say. *Your features have been blurred by a film.* The words were on his tongue, and he swallowed them. Piper's voice was still rough with the remnants of last night; he couldn't kill the spell by complaining.

Instead, he focused on her face with all his might, hoping that by sheer will, he could bring it into focus. "I'm fine," he said. "I'm still waking up."

"Well, then go into the dining room and I'll get us some coffee. I told Joan—I mean, Mrs. Lester—I'd make more breakfast potatoes, but I'm sure she won't mind if I back out to eat with you. After all, I am a guest."

"No, don't." Frederic wasn't ready to navigate breakfast yet. "That is, I need to get something at the apothecary first."

"Do you want me to come with you?"

Yes. Please. "Why don't you help Mrs. Lester? I will be back as soon as I can, and we'll have breakfast then."

"Okay."

He couldn't help himself. He needed contact, to reassure himself everything would be all right. Cupping her face, he kissed her, tasting her as though it were his last taste. *Which is could very well be.*

"Whoa, cowboy," Piper said with a laugh. "You're going to spill the coffee. Go run your errand. We can finish what you started when you get back."

The sun was already bright when Frederic stepped outside. He'd hoped the light would improve things, but no. If anything, the colors were more muted.

He wished he had thought to count the steps yesterday. He remembered turning right and crossing the street at the corner, but after that…

A car horn blared, forcing him back on the curb.

Frederic, you arrogant idiot. This wasn't Paris, where he knew every street with perfect familiarity. This was a strange village in a foreign country. A town made up of identical stone facades that, thanks to the film, blurred into one giant building. He scanned the storefronts looking for a sign that would tell him his location.

"Pardon," he murmured as he bumped a woman's shoulder. "Excuse me," he said when he bumped into another. He couldn't look where he was heading and read the store signs. If he had Piper come with him she could have…

…helped.

Disgusted with himself, he stopped in his tracks.

"Your butter is browning."

Shoot. Piper snatched the frying pan off the burner, but it was too late. The butter was already dark. "Sorry. I lost track of what I was doing."

"You do seem a little out of sorts," the innkeeper replied. She reached over and took the frying pan from Piper's grip, before gently pushing her backward away from the stove. "I'll tell you what," she said. "You're not in a cooking mood today, so how about I do the potatoes and you finish your coffee and wake up."

Piper didn't really have much choice but to agree. Mrs. Lester was right; her head wasn't into cooking.

"You know…" the innkeeper was saying, "I don't know how they do things at that fancy cooking school of yours, but here in England, we get a good night's rest if we're cooking in the morning." Her lecture came with a twinkling smile. "You new lovers always think you can burn the candle at both ends, don't you?"

"Since I'm not an employee, I'm technically only burning one end," Piper shot back. She pointedly ignored the lovers comment. Was that what she and Frederic were? Lovers? The word sounded so sex-based, and what they shared last night was so much more. It had been for Piper, anyway. Her feelings had shifted while standing on that hill behind the abbey. Just how much, she was still too afraid to say.

It wasn't her late-night activities that were destroying her concentration, however. It was her morning conversation. She couldn't put her finger on why, but something about Frederic was different. He wasn't the same man who reached for her in the middle of the night. Since he stepped outside, Piper had been racking her brain trying to think whether she'd crossed a line and said too much. Maybe her emotions weren't as hidden as she thought. Maybe she was too obvious, and he was worried she wouldn't be able to handle this no-strings relationship they had going on.

That would certainly explain why his kiss felt strangely like goodbye.

On the other hand, maybe she was being a paranoid loon. Frederic was going to a drugstore, for goodness' sake. He probably had a headache.

Meanwhile, Mrs. Lester had taken over cooking duties, giving Piper a silent lesson in bed-and-breakfast cooking.

"Would you like me to sit in the dining room out of your way?" she asked.

"Goodness, no. I like your company. I don't let just anyone in my kitchen, you know." Picking up a nearby cutting board, the woman scraped a pile of diced onions into a heated fry pan. The vegetables crackled, filling the room with aroma. "What were we talking about, anyway?"

"You were giving me your recipe for Cornish pasties."

"Right. Although I'm surprised that someone

studying haute cuisine would be interested in making something like hand pies."

"For your information, I happen to like hand pies," Piper shot back.

"I can cook them a lot better than haute cuisine, that's for sure," she added, speaking to the inside of her cup.

"What did you say?"

"Nothing." Now wasn't the time or place to go into her problems with Chef Despelteau. "I'm in a comfort food phase, is all."

"Can't blame you there. I've been in one my whole life. The mister took me to eat in London on my birthday last year. A couple medallions of beef drowned in sauce and an itty-bitty dollop of risotto. Seems to me, if you're going to charge fifty pounds for dinner, a person shouldn't need a snack when she gets home."

"I totally agree," Piper said. One of her pet peeves about Chef Despelteau was his emphasis on presentation instead of serving size. "I was telling Frederic the other night that sauces are great, but sometimes a steak should be left a steak." She paused to take a sip of coffee. "Good comfort food isn't all that easy to make, either. Half the time the restaurants try to trendy it up, and end up getting it all wrong."

"Like up at the Hen & Rooster. That's why I prefer the old-fashioned pubs. Give me fish and chips any day."

"Same here," Piper said. "Same here."

"Then why are you in that class?" Mrs. Lester asked.

"I beg your pardon?"

The woman shrugged one of her shoulders. "Seems to me if you don't like fancy foods, you shouldn't be in some fancy French school. So why are you?"

Why did everyone ask her the same question?

She had only herself to blame this time. She had opened the door by talking about comfort food.

"Because I want to become a chef, and where better to learn than in Paris?" Her answer sounded flat even to her this time. She was tired. Frederic kept her up half the night. Plus, she was tired of justifying herself.

Justifying yourself or justifying to yourself?

"Well, I suppose if you want the prestige…"

At Mrs. Lester's comment, she shook off the strange thought. "Of course English cooking is pretty awesome, too." She didn't mean to hurt the woman's feelings. "That's why I want to make Cornish pasties."

"Mine do get a lot of compliments," Mrs. Lester said, smiling. "But so you know, Cornish pasties are Welsh, not English. You don't want to be messing up the two."

"Yes, ma'am."

Just then, the front doorbell rang, signaling an arrival. "I'll get that," she told Mrs. Lester. "It's probably Frederic back from his walk." At least she hoped so. His odd goodbye continued to plague her. "Would you mind writing down your recipe so I can take it back with me?"

"Of course I can," Mrs. Lester replied. "Soon

as I finish breakfast, I'll do it. Oh, and if that is a guest, let them know the rooms don't turn over until after twelve. They can leave their luggage in the tea room."

"Will do." Piper had to laugh. Apparently, over the weekend she'd become an employee, only no one told her.

It was Frederic, all right. He stood at the base of the stairs, staring down at his shoes. As lost and distant as she had ever seen him.

Don't overreact. There could be lots of reasons why he didn't go to the kitchen himself.

"Did you get what you needed from the store?" she asked him.

"No. I didn't go."

He didn't? Where had he been, then? As she stepped closer, Piper saw his hand had the banister in a vise grip. His was squeezing the wood so hard his knuckles were white.

"I've got a headache," he said. "I'm going to lie down."

"I'll go with you." She hurried to catch up

with him, her fingers brushing his elbow as she reached the bottom step.

Frederic stiffened at her touch. "No," he told her. "I don't need anyone keeping me company." With one hand on the wall and one hand on the rail, he walked slowly upstairs.

Her stomach felt as if it had been kicked.

Pushing her fear aside, she headed upstairs to find out what happened.

She found Frederic sitting on the edge of the unmade bed, staring into space. His head didn't so much as turn when she closed the door. "I thought you were going to lie down."

"I changed my mind."

"Would you like me to see if Mrs. Lester has any aspirin?"

"No, thank you. I will be fine."

The change in his voice frightened her. Last night's warmth had disappeared in favor of a tone so polite and distant it hurt her ears. She hadn't heard him use that voice since the days when she first started work. Back when they'd been strangers.

Where was the man who was whispering sweet nothings in the dark a few hours ago? She raced through everything they said and did yesterday, wondering what could have happened to make him disappear so abruptly.

Oh, no... Not that. It hadn't even been twenty-four hours...

"It's your eyes, isn't it?"

Frederic stood up, only to stand stock-still, as if he wasn't sure where to go. "Yes."

"Oh, Frederic." It wasn't fair. She hugged him from behind, holding him as tightly as possible. Letting him know best she could that he wasn't alone, and that he could lean on her in any way he needed to. Frederic's body was rigid. Even with their bodies pressed together, it felt as if he were a million miles away. He was in shock. Who could blame him? Even the most prepared man would need time to adjust.

"Everything will be all right," she told him. Ignoring the hairs rising on the back of her neck, she kissed his shoulder blade. "I'm here, and I'll do whatever you need me to do."

For a moment, she felt Frederic's body relax as he leaned against her. Before the moment could take hold, however, he stepped away, leaving her standing alone at the foot of the bed.

"I have to pack," he said. "Can you let Mrs. Lester know we're checking out?"

It couldn't have sounded more like she was being dismissed if he had tried.

CHAPTER NINE

IT WAS LATE when they returned to Paris. Frederic called ahead to his doctor, and the man met them at the hospital. To run tests, he said. Personally Frederic thought it a waste of time. What would a battery of tests show that his eyes couldn't tell him already?

Now that the shock had time to wear off, he was coming to terms with his new reality: his vision had deteriorated again, and while he wasn't completely blind, he was much, much closer. The translucent film draping his view wasn't going away. He would never see sharply again. Only a matter of time before he woke up and his sight was gone forever.

He always knew this day would come—the day he moved another step closer to blindness. His eyes getting worse had always been a matter of when, not if. He only hoped to have more time. With Piper, that is.

Frederic closed his eyes. After the catastrophe in the village, he had managed to rally fairly well. Until Saint Pancras station with its crowds and low lighting. The confusion made his head pound. If not for Piper playing guide dog… *Watch your step. Turn left. Wait here.* Her voice echoed in his ear, steady and soft. Like the woman herself. A calm in his storm.

It was so easy to hand over control. Terrifyingly so. More terrifying was the security he felt when she linked her arm with his. He followed her lead with complete trust, knowing that if something went wrong, she would be by his side.

Finally, after all these years, he understood how his father had become so needy. Surrendering control—the peace that came from surrendering control, that is—was addictive. Why not let someone else carry the burden, especially when they offered things like goodness and light in return?

He couldn't do that to Piper. Life had dragged her down enough.

At least he would always have yesterday at the abbey.

The sound of sandals flapping caused his pulse to speed up. He already knew the sound of her walk, he thought dejectedly. So much for his goal of a quick, unencumbered affair.

The curtain drew back. "You've got to love Paris. The hospital cafeteria has better pastries than most American bakeries. I brought you a croissant. Do you want it in front of you or...?"

"Leave it on the side table."

"Are you sure? You haven't eaten all day."

"I think I would know if I was hungry." The words came out far sharper than he meant. She had no idea her kindness made things worse. "I'm sorry," he said. "I didn't mean..."

"You've had a long day."

"So have you."

"I'll live."

"It's late. You should go back to the house."

"Not so late," she said, pulling one of the plastic chairs closer to the bed. The metal legs scraped against the floor with a loud *squeak*. "At some point, Dr. Doucette will release you, and we'll go home together."

The idea of the two of them as a team left Frederic warm all over. Another warning bell. "I'd rather you left now. I'll have Michel drive me home later."

"Don't be silly. I'm sure Dr. Doucette will be here very soon."

"Piper, I want you to go." This time, he didn't mince words.

There was no mistaking Piper's confusion. "You don't want me here?"

Exactly the opposite. Frederic wanted her by his side so badly it hurt. "I think it would be a good idea if you left," he told her.

"I see."

For several minutes, she stared at the floor.

Frederic assumed she was angry, and after she'd taken a couple long, clearing breaths, she would leave. Thus, when her hand settled over his, he started. "You're not alone," she said. "You know that, right?"

That was the whole point. He wasn't, but if he was any kind of decent human being, he would be. He should have never pursued her in the first place. But no, he'd been selfish, thinking with his desire, not with his head. Warmth spread up Frederic's arm, mocking his already-aching heart. If he let her stay, he would lean on her. And lean, and lean and lean.

He would never let her go.

"Please go, Piper. You are not obligated to stay here." Painful as it was, he tried to pull his fingers free of her grip. She surprised him by holding on with ferocity, as though she was the person leaning on him.

"Yes, I am," she said. "I know we haven't been together very long, but I…"

"Don't." He didn't want her to say something

that couldn't be forgotten. A sentiment that would make the inevitable that much harder.

Forcing his voice to stay as even as possible, he said the words that really needed to be said. "We had a good time together, but we both knew from the start that this was a short-term relationship. No promises."

"No strings. Thanks for reminding me." At last, she yanked her hand free, the loss of contact traveling straight to his chest. "Funny how you decided tonight is the perfect night to cut me loose. Here I thought that after last night… What happened to having an unforgettable couple of months?"

Frederic dropped his gaze to the sheet. Ironic that even with his deteriorated vision, he couldn't look her in the eye. He knew that even the gauzy haze couldn't obliterate the hurt he would see there. "Last night we were both carried away. Now that I have had a chance to think clearly, I've come to realize that the longer we continue this affair, the harder goodbye will be. We should make things easy by ending it while we both have happy memories."

"Easy on who? Me or you?"

"Both of us."

She let out a derisive snort. "Right."

The chair legs scraped across the linoleum as she stood up. Her sandals made angry slaps as she paced the floor. "Tell me something, Frederic. Would you have come to this decision if you hadn't woken up this morning with your eye problem?"

Denying the truth would only insult her. "No."

"I didn't think so. Honestly, do you think I care that your eyes got worse?"

"I care." And while she might not now, she would come to resent it, and by extension, him. "I would rather you remember me fondly."

"No problem. Dumping me is the perfect way to do that."

"Better I dump you than drag you down."

"Drag me…? Is that what you think would happen?"

It was what he *knew* would happen. Last night he had promised her romance. "It's not very romantic if your lover can't see."

"Except as you've pointed out many times, you can."

"But at some point I won't. Today was a reminder of that fact. That is why we would be smart to end things now. Before either of us gets too attached." He refused to listen to the voice telling him it was too late.

"What if I don't want to? End it, that is."

Frederic sighed. *Stubborn woman.* He accepted that this was the way it was supposed to be; why couldn't she?

His eyes searched the room until he found her standing near the foot of his bed. Staring straight at her, he spoke with great deliberation, to make sure she understood. "You don't have a choice. This is for the best."

"Says you."

She didn't move. She stood at the foot of the bed, with her eyes bearing down on him. Frederic could feel their wounded glare. "You're wrong, you know. You wouldn't drag me down."

You say that now... "I have no doubt my mother said the same thing to my father." And look how well that turned out. A woman so broken from taking care of the man, she wasn't able to live a life for herself. A son who grew up never respecting the man who fathered him. "I'm not going to be selfish enough to make the same mistake." Not with Piper or anyone else.

"Even though you can see, and I'm scheduled to go back to Boston in a couple months."

They both knew if their affair continued, he wouldn't be able to let her return to Boston. The feelings between them were already deeper than a mere affair. "Even though," he replied.

Through his haze, he saw that Piper was trembling; she was fighting to keep herself from crying. Keeping her pride. Admiration swelled in his chest, along with deeper, unmentionable emotions. Someday she would thank him.

"You deserve nothing but the best, Piper." He meant every blessed word.

"Go to hell."

Frederic listened to the slap of her sandals until he couldn't hear them anymore before giving in to the frustration gnawing at his insides and punching at the bed as hard as he could. As moments went, this was not his finest.

I did the right thing. What would prolonging the affair do other than make the pain of saying goodbye worse? At least this way, her heart wasn't so damaged it wouldn't heal. She would meet someone else, a man who wouldn't grow to need her quite so much.

Dammit! His chest felt as if someone had torn it open. Who knew you could fall so hard so fast?

He should have. He should have realized it the other night in his kitchen when his body was on fire and his head was warning him that Piper wasn't like other women. All he could do was dream of making love to her. This... He punched the bed again, this time hitting the side rail so hard it rattled. This was his punishment for being selfish.

At least he would have a lifetime of solitude to get over his mistake.

"Is everything all right?" A nurse suddenly appeared in the doorway from which Piper just left. "Monsieur, do you need anything?"

Frederic stared blankly at the space across the room. "No," he replied. "I don't need anything."

Better to break things off before either of us becomes too attached, Frederic had said.

Too late. Piper made it as far as the taxi before giving in to her tears. The driver stared at her through his rearview mirror as tears streamed down her face.

"Mademoiselle?" he asked in a soft voice. "Are you all right?"

"Fine," she replied, sniffling.

A moment later, the safety glass slid back and he handed her a tissue through the opening. Seeing it reminded her of how Frederic offered her a paper towel, and she burst into a fresh batch. "Thank you," she managed to choke out between sniffs.

Damn Frederic Lafontaine. Why couldn't he have left her alone and miserable? Why did he have to decide to get involved in her art search and make her fall for him? Now instead of lonely and miserable, she was brokenhearted and miserable.

Here she thought living in Paris couldn't feel worse.

She blew her nose. Frederic was wrong, too. Two days, eight weeks—the length of their affair didn't matter because she had already fallen in deep. What she felt for him went way beyond lust or romantic fantasy. She loved him. With all her soul. Blind, sighted, purple, green, two-headed… none of that mattered. The part she loved was inside. The tender, intelligent man who loved art and history, and who made her feel as though she could do anything.

Stupid her, she thought Frederic felt the same. Really stupid her, she still thought it.

Surely she didn't imagine the feelings between them last night. Frederic said himself that they would still be together had his eyes not gotten worse this morning.

All because of his parents. Why was it that parents always screwed things up for their kids? Her mom's leaving Patience and her to survive on their own. Frederic's parents' making him think his disease was better suffered alone. If Frederic's parents were alive, she'd kill them for turning their son into a self-sacrificing idiot. Why couldn't he see that he wasn't like his father? The Frederic she knew was far too strong to let blindness beat him, if and when he finally lost his sight.

So what now? Suck it up and soldier on as she always did? How was she supposed to go back to being Frederic's housekeeper after the last two days? Simply being in the same room as him made her pulse race. No way could she live in the same house.

She'd have to move out, she realized, letting out a sigh. Move out and find some place cheap to finish out the term. Great. Twenty-four hours ago she was wrapped in Frederic's arms, listening to him sleep and dreaming of the days ahead. Now she was on the brink of homelessness with nothing to look forward to but days filled with being lectured by Chef Despelteau.

She wished she'd never come to Paris.

Who was she kidding? If she hadn't come to Paris, she wouldn't have met Frederic, and lousy as she felt, she wouldn't have traded the past five days for anything.

Then fight for them. Patience's voice was loud in her head. *Figure out a way to fix the situation.*

Her sister was right. Wasn't the whole point of coming to Paris so that she could achieve her dreams? Frederic was part of those dreams now.

She wasn't walking away without a fight.

CHAPTER TEN

SHE WAS IN the kitchen waiting on a pan of brownies when Frederic finally returned home. "What are you doing?" he asked.

The day had been hard on him. His face was pale and drawn, with dark circles under his eyes. She moved to take him in her arms, then stopped. Any compassion she offered would only get rejected.

She returned to the sink and the bowl she was washing out. "Making brownies. They'll be ready in a few minutes if you want to wait."

"I wasn't expecting you to be here."

"Where else would I be? This is my job. Unless I'm fired, too," she added, turning the bowl upside down.

From behind her, she heard him let out a long sigh. "Why would you want to stay?"

For you. "Because I've already done homeless once in my life. I don't feel like doing it again."

"I wouldn't let that happen. I'll pay for you to stay at a hotel or find a new apartment."

"Would you find me a new job, too?"

"We would find some kind of arrangement."

"Wonderful. In other words, you'll pay me to stay away." The oven timer rang. "If it's all the same to you, I'll finish out my contract here," she said, reaching for the oven mitt.

"I know what you're doing," he said. "Staying won't make me change my mind."

"Then it shouldn't be a problem for you." Dropping the pan of brownies on the cooling rack, she waited for him to mount a new argument. Dared him to.

"It won't work," he said. "I'm going to bed. Dr Doucette wants to meet with me before I go to the university."

"What for?" Did something show up in the tests they ran today?

"To fit me for a white cane, I presume. He mentioned something about transition lessons. I won't need breakfast."

The last part meant to remind her she was back to being a housekeeper. Very well, she'd let him have his way tonight. She sighed. "Yes, sir."

As it turned out, Frederic found a reason to not need breakfast or dinner the next two days. For all she saw of him, he might have been the one who took a room at a hotel. Not that he ignored her. No, he talked to her when their paths crossed. Politely worded requests about laundry and other household business. In other words, they'd turned back the clock to when she was simply his housekeeper.

On the third morning, she found him asleep in his chair.

He must have come home very late. She'd waited until well after midnight before going to her rooms.

For a few minutes, Piper contented herself with simply watching him sleep. Kind of on the obsessive side, she knew, but she couldn't help herself. She hadn't had a good look at his face in two days, and she needed to see how he was doing.

In England, she had noticed how Frederic's features would relax while sleeping. His lips would part in a smile as if he was dreaming happy thoughts. There was no smile today. His face was drawn tight. "You foolish man," she whispered. "We could be sleeping together."

A lock of his hair hung over his eye. She brushed it aside, letting her fingers linger on his face. Felt so wonderful to touch him again. It might have been only two days, but it seemed like an eternity.

Frederic stirred. "Mmm, nice," he said in a drowsy voice.

This was the Frederic she knew in England. Stuck between sleep and consciousness, he hadn't raised his defenses yet. Piper's hear ached for his reappearance. "You fell asleep in the chair again."

"I was watching the tower."

With his eyes still closed, he curved into her touch, catching her hand in his and pressing a kiss to the palm. Piper gave a soft sigh. *I missed you.*

His eyes fluttered open. The defenses returned. "Piper..."

She lifted her hand away, but it didn't matter. The moment was there, between them. Frederic could protest all he wanted, but it was clear that the feelings they discovered in England weren't about to go away.

"Nothing's changed," he said, pushing to his feet.

"I can tell," Piper replied.

"That's not what I meant, and you know it." She watched as he stalked his way to his favorite window. He stood with his hands pressed against the molding, the muscles in his shoulders playing beneath his jacket as he attempted to push the wooden frame apart. "This isn't going to work," he said. "You staying here. Let me…"

"Find a hotel? No, thanks."

"For God's sake," he said, spinning around to face her again. "Why are you being so stubborn?"

"Why are you?"

When he didn't answer, Piper stepped closer. "Tell you what." She kept her eyes locked with his, so he would be sure to see the determination on her face. "I will leave if you can honestly tell me you don't care about me as much as I care about you."

Frederic looked away. "You know I can't."

Piper's heart skipped a beat.

"But," he said, raising his eyes again, "that doesn't mean we have a future. Not even a short-term one. I can't."

Good Lord, but she was tired of hearing the word *can't*. He most definitely could, if he let himself. "What are you so scared of?"

"I'm not scared of anything."

"Liar. I think you're terrified. You're afraid of the day you wake up and can't see anymore."

"That's where you're wrong. I've been expecting to go blind since I was fifteen years old. I know exactly how my life will play out."

"And how is that?" she challenged.

"Alone."

He said the word with such finality, it ripped her insides in two. Did he really believe that he was meant to be by himself for the rest of his days? How could one man be so incredibly wrong?

"It doesn't have to be that way," she said.

"Yes, it does. I've known that since I was fifteen years old, too. I will never turn the life of the person I...I care about upside down the way my father did ours."

"Even if the person is willing to take the risk?" She touched his wrist, offering.

"It's always easy to be willing at the beginning. It becomes obligation."

"Not necessarily."

"Says the woman who is attending a school she hates because she owes her sister."

Piper stepped back. "That's not true."

"Isn't it?" Frederic asked. "Then tell me when the last time was that you enjoyed cooking?"

When she made him pot roast.

"Do you even like French food?"

"What does that matter?" she countered. "People cook things they don't like all the time." Why were they talking about school all of a sudden, anyway? This wasn't about her.

Narrowing his eyes, Frederic stared down at her with so much intensity it made her insides squirm. "The other night you asked me 'what if' to prove your point, remember? Now it is my turn. What if Patience hadn't been so excited about you going to Paris? What if she hadn't sacrificed so much? Would you still be here?"

"I…" She couldn't say the answer aloud.

"That's what I thought. You're so determined to give back to your sister. Have you ever asked if she cared what you did for a living?"

"She sacrificed for me to be here."

"No, she sacrificed for you to have a *good life.* You were the one who decided that meant being a French chef."

"Not true." France was both their dreams. Hers and Patience's. Frederic was using this as an excuse.

"You can keep telling yourself that all you want, but I will not be another person to whom you feel obligated."

"For crying out loud, Frederic, *I'm not your mother.* Don't treat me like I am." It was the only argument she had left.

Like all her other arguments, it fell on deaf ears. "Finish your school and go home, Piper," he said as he brushed past her.

Piper gnawed the inside of her cheek as she watched him make his way to the staircase. How dare he twist her argument against her? Cooking school was an entirely different situation. For starters, she and Patience dreamed this dream together, meaning it was 50 percent her sister's. Maybe 60 percent. Or 70.

Stupid "what-if" games. Sinking into the chair, she threw her head back to stare at the ceiling. Maybe she was sticking it out because of Patience. If she hadn't, though, she never would have started her affair with Frederic. And wanting to be with him was 100 percent her idea. There wasn't a drop of obligation involved.

Of course, she could see how that might be hard to believe. Why would he think she was sticking with him by choice if her Paris track record said otherwise?

What should she do now? Maybe Patience…

She stopped halfway to her pocket. No. The solution had to be her own. Besides, there was nothing Patience could say that Piper hadn't heard a hundred times before. *Go for your dreams. You can do anything. I just want you to be happy.*

Happy.

That had always been her sister's dream: for Piper to be happy. *So long as you're happy, there it's all worthwhile,* she used to say whenever Piper felt guilty.

She wasn't happy in culinary school. *Face it, Piper, you'd rather be cooking mac and cheese instead of foie gras.*

Was it any wonder her assignments were uninspired? She didn't love making them the way she loved making good old-fashioned comfort food. If she wanted to be brutally honest, she'd been going through the motions the past couple months. Frederic was right; she might have come to Paris on her own, but she'd stayed out of obligation to her sister. Patience would smack her if she knew.

Suddenly Piper was very disgusted with herself.

But it wasn't the same when it came to Frederic. Being with him, being needed by him, could never be an obligation. She didn't fall in love with his ability to see. She fell in love with the man who accepted his blindness and survived anyway.

How could she make him see that they weren't doomed to repeat his parents' mistakes?

The first step would be to get her own life in order.

"Leave?" Chef Despelteau said. "There are only eight weeks left in the program."

"I know," Piper replied. "Trust me, this wasn't an easy decision."

That wasn't true. Actually, the decision had been very easy, once she thought everything through.

The best way to thank Patience wasn't struggling to become something she wasn't simply because she was afraid she would let down Patience. In fact, just the opposite. She was letting Patience down by being so unhappy. If she wanted to truly thank her sister, she should create a life she loved. Cooking would be part of that dream. Just not French cooking.

"I've decided to take my cooking in a different direction," she told Chef Despelteau.

"I am very sorry to hear that. You had the potential to be a great French chef."

Piper smiled. His attempt at sincerity was uninspired.

She left his office feeling a hundred pounds
lighter. Now if she could only get through to
Frederic, then she would be truly happy.

Frederic was there when she returned home. He
was standing by his window as usual. Something
about it felt off, though. It didn't take long for her
to realize what. Propped against the wall was a
white-and-red cane. "Dr. Doucette wants me to
use it when I'm walking around the city to avoid
accidents," he said when she asked about it. He
didn't say anything further.

Leaving the floor open for her announcement.
"I quit culinary school."

Frederic turned away from the window to look
at her. "You what?"

"You were right," she told him. "The only reason I was staying was because I thought I owed

Patience. I realized that was wrong. She would never want me to do something that made me miserable out of obligation. She would want me to choose what made me happy."

"Oh."

That was it? She thought he would show a little more reaction. Maybe not jump up and down, but something more than a flat monosyllable.

"I assume that means you'll be leaving for home soon, then," he said. There was a strange note to his voice that Piper couldn't decide was disappointment or relief.

She certainly knew the emotion deadening her stomach. "No, I'm not leaving," she said. "Don't you understand? I quit because I know the difference between doing something for obligation and choosing something I want to do. *I know the difference.*

"I also know what makes me happy." What she wanted to say next was important. She cupped his face in her hands, so he had no choice but to look her in the eye. "You make me happy, Fred-

eric. For months I was miserable. I hated Paris—
I hated school. Then you shoved a paper towel
in front of my face and everything changed. I
wasn't miserable anymore."

"Piper—"

"Let me finish. Do you know what made me so
happy? It wasn't dancing by the river or a whirl-
wind trip to the English countryside. It wasn't
just physical, either. It was sitting next to you
on the train and listening to you complain that
England had terrible coffee. It was hearing you
explain why you loved that God-awful mural.
It was being with you. You were all I needed to
make Paris worthwhile."

She could see his defenses crumbling. The
cracks showed in his eyes. "Everyone feels that
way at the start of a new romance," he said.
"You'll get over it."

"I don't want to get over it. I don't want to get
over you. I'm falling in love with you."

She kissed him, letting her lips do the rest of
he talking for her, and for a moment, as he kissed

her back, everything slid back into place. *Say you don't love me back, Frederic. I dare you.*

His hands reached up to cover hers and gently pulled them away. "Then walk away," he whispered. "Don't let me drain you dry."

"Damn you!" Damn him *and* his parents. She shoved at his chest, then shoved again. "I am so sick of your dumbass self-sacrificing. For what? Because your parents had a bad marriage? Because your dad was a needy jerk? Did you ever stop to think that maybe it wasn't helping your father that burned your mother out, it was his constantly feeling sorry for himself? News flash Frederic. You're acting as badly as he ever did."

"I am not my father."

"Oh, that's right. You're not going to drag anyone down with you. No, you'll just shove aside anyone who cares about you. To hell with what they want."

Frederic didn't answer. He looked past her, to the tower, his expression more distant than ever

They were back where they began. Two people, separate and alone.

Piper was done. What fight she had left disappeared as soon as she saw his expression. Some situations couldn't be fixed, no matter how hard you tried.

"I'm going to Gloucestershire," she told him. The backup plan she hoped to never use. "Mrs. Lester said I was welcome to come and cook any time I wanted—I'm going to take her up on the offer. I'll be packed and out of here by the end of the day."

Halfway across the room, she paused, unable to help one parting shot.

"There's a difference between needing help and self-pity, you know. Too bad you're too blind to see it. But then, maybe you're too blind to see a lot of things."

Leaving him to his solitude, she went to her room and packed. Frederic never came to say goodbye. She didn't expect him to.

The Eiffel Tower greeted her as she stepped

onto the sidewalk. Tall and gray, it would forever be her symbol of Paris. A reminder of both the best and worst of her time in this city. Taking out her cell phone, she took one last picture.

And said goodbye.

Time, Frederic decided, was playing tricks on him. When he was with Piper, time whipped by. Their few days together were over before he realized. So how was it the forty-eight hours since Piper moved out had stretched endlessly?

Oh, he was busy enough. He had his classes to teach, and classes to take. The life transition classes Dr. Doucette suggested. There were the social and professional obligations that kept him out until late at night. His eyesight might have dropped another notch, but his lifestyle hadn't missed a beat. There was only one problem: he missed Piper.

At night, he would lie in bed and remember the afternoon at the abbey. The way her eyes had looked so blue as he hovered above her. Frederic cherished the memory. It had been his last day of clear sight, and life had blessed him with a wonderful view. Funny, he always thought the visual memory he'd long for most would be some piece of art. Or the tower, perhaps. His trusty friend, whose lights twinkled invitingly, albeit a little hazier now.

No. It was the memory of Piper's eyes that he prayed he'd never forget. He wouldn't trade the memory of her eyes for a thousand Eiffel Towers.

God, he missed her. Breathing hurt without her. The air was too thin, and his shirt collars were always strangling him. He missed her voice. He missed her smell. He missed her touch. And who did he have to blame? No one but himself.

Thanks to him, she was in a completely different country, charming the locals with her bright smile. He bet she was making plans for her return to America right now, too. All because he was afraid she would bail when things got hard.

You fool. He could have had Piper in his life

for as long as she'd have him. Instead, he didn't have her at all.

There's a difference between needing help and self-pity, Piper told him. His father had needed *so* much. He remembered when he was a kid, wanting to go to the tower, but his father had refused because of the crowds. *I can't handle all those people*, he'd said. And so Frederic had gone with the nanny while his mother stayed home, because his father didn't want to be alone. The man couldn't handle being by himself any more than he could handle being with people.

Was there ever a day when his father didn't remind them he couldn't see? How many family events did they miss? How many holidays had to be rearranged? His father wore his blindness like a shield and demanded that it—no, *he*—be acknowledged at every turn.

Had Frederic done the same? Was his insistence on bearing the burden alone a different version of the same self-absorption?

Exhaling long and slow, he closed his eyes. His

brain still believed breaking up with Piper was the right thing to do. His heart, on the other hand, needed her. He'd tried listening to his brain, and as a result, he was sitting in a giant house by himself while his heart threatened to break in half.

It didn't have to be this way. He could go to England.

Then what? Beg her to come back, and risk her falling out of love with him?

Better to risk than to live as he had the last forty-eight hours. Piper made the days worthwhile. Without her, they were simply days.

It was time he listened to his heart.

"So I said to myself, why are you playing hardball? There is no reason why you should be hangin' on to that gorgeous painting when Ana Duchenko is in Boston, heartbroken and alone. You can tell her nephew I am more than willing to sell."

Digging into the paper bag he set on the table earlier, John Allen pulled out a blueberry scone.

Immediately, Mrs. Lester scoffed. "I'll have you know, there's a perfectly good scone right here."

"I'm sure you make a wonderful scone, but these are gluten-free. I make them with my own flour mix. Try one."

The innkeeper pinched a bite from the pastry on his plate. "Not bad," she said, chewing slowly. "Not as good as mine, but not bad. Do you want to try some, Piper? Piper?"

"Huh?" Piper looked up from her coffee to find John and Mrs. Lester staring at her.

"Sorry," Piper said. "I'm trying to concentrate, but my head doesn't want to cooperate." It was too busy thinking about a stubborn idiot who didn't—no who *couldn't*—love her.

"Still out of sorts, are ya?"

"Afraid so." She was beginning to think she would be out of sorts forever. "Maybe I should have stayed in Paris."

"And do what?" the older woman asked. "Finish at that snooty cooking school?"

"No. Chef Despelteau and I parted ways for

good." Quitting school was the one decision Piper didn't regret. Frederic was right; Patience didn't care whether she stayed enrolled or not. On her way out of Paris, Piper had texted her sister and asked that very question.

All I've ever cared about is you being happy, whatever you decide to do, her sister had texted back. Is everything okay?

Piper gave her one last lie and said everything was fine. This time it wasn't to appease her sister, but to avoid feeling worse. Her sister and Stuart had repaired their relationship and were in a serious honeymoon phase. Piper was afraid hearing the happiness in her sister's voice would cause her to break down.

"I don't think it's the school she's missing," John said.

"I keep thinking if I stayed in Paris, I might have been able to convince Frederic he was being a stubborn idiot." She couldn't believe how much she loved him after such a short time.

"People gotta work out their demons for themselves," Mrs. Lester said. "You stickin' around waiting on him won't make the process go any faster."

"True." In a way, staying where she wasn't wanted would be as bad as staying out of obligation.

Staying with Mrs. Lester might have been a mistake as well. Everywhere she looked she saw some kind of reminder of the weekend she spent with Frederic. Even the damn kitchen wasn't safe. Nights were worse. She lay in bed reliving the ones they had shared.

"Why don't you come stay with me?" John said when Mrs. Lester went to answer the front doorbell. "We could experiment with grain-free recipes."

Piper smiled. "You are a very sweet man, Mr. Allen, but I think I'm better off staying here." Perverse as it was.

"For the last time, call me John, and if you change your mind, the offer will always be there. It's the least I can do for a fellow Ana lover."

Just then, Mrs. Lester called from the front hallway. "Piper? Could you come here a minute, dear? I need you for something."

"Coming, Mrs. Lester."

She found the innkeeper standing at the base of the stairs waiting for her. The older woman had the oddest expression on her face. "Is something wrong?" she asked.

"You tell me," Mrs. Lester replied, nodding her head toward the entryway.

Piper gasped. "Frederic?"

She couldn't believe her eyes. Was he really standing in Mrs. Lester's doorway?

At the sound of her voice, he took off his sunglasses. Piper saw that his hand was trembling. He looked as bad as she felt, with circles turning his eyes dark and gloomy.

"What are you doing here?" she asked.

"You were right," he said. "I *was* blind."

"You were?" She had to ask to make sure she wasn't dreaming. When she walked out of his house, she was certain she would never see Frederic again. Now he was here, and echoing the words she left behind… It was all too unreal.

Frederic stepped closer, stopping just short of her arms. "I thought the only way I could avoid being like my father was to shut myself off. If I didn't need anyone, then I couldn't drive them away. I didn't see that…" He let out a breath. "I thought I was protecting you. Instead I was doing exactly what I swore I would never do. And that was drive the woman I love away."

"Do you mean that?" Out of the corner of her eye, she saw Mrs. Lester disappearing into the kitchen to give them privacy. It was just her, Frederic and the declaration he made.

"That I love you? More than I thought possible. And I was an idiot for pushing you away. You are the best thing that has ever happened to me, Piper. I never should have let you walk out the door. Can you ever forgive me?"

"I…" She wanted to laugh and cry at the same time. Could she forgive him? "You put me through hell," she reminded him.

"I know, love. And I understand if you can't forgive me. I took too long to come to my senses." He lowered his head. "Perhaps if I hadn't been so stubborn…"

"I can't believe you came to England," Piper said. She wasn't quite ready to forgive him, but she also didn't want him to leave.

"I would have gone twice as far. I had to come. I had to let you know that while I don't deserve your forgiveness—not for one second—I…I need you."

That was all she needed to hear. Before he could say another word, Piper was in his arms, lost to the warmth of his embrace.

"I missed you so much," he whispered against her cheek. "My world was dark without you. Please, please tell me you forgive me."

"I forgive you," she whispered back. She had to squeeze her eyes shut to keep the tears back.

Frederic's eyes were as wet as hers. "There's a lot we have to work out. Being with a blind man isn't going to be easy."

"I know."

"There might be days when the frustration gets to me, and I become a selfish boor."

It wasn't funny, but Piper had to laugh. "You mean more so than these past few days?"

"I only want to make you happy."

"Then…" She took his hand. "Then be strong enough to let me help you. Don't push me away."

"Never again," he said. "But you have to promise that if you are ever unhappy…"

"I will let you know, and we'll work on a solution together."

"I love you, Piper Rush, and I want…no, I *need* you by my side." Cradling her face, he kissed her, a kiss so much like the one they shared at the abbey, and Piper gave up battling the tears.

"Please don't cry, love," he said, wiping at the dampness. "This is a happy time. Besides, I don' have a handkerchief."

"Maybe we can steal a paper towel from Mrs Lester," she said with a laugh. It felt good to fee light again after all these days. She sniffed back as many tears as she could. "And I am happy. More than you can imagine."

Frederic looked wonderful in his tuxedo. He balked at renting one at first, but Piper insisted. *If I'm wearing a gown, then you're wearing a tuxedo,* she told him. After all, the man was born to wear black tie. Especially for his wedding.

It wasn't a real wedding ceremony. Two weeks was way too soon for any kind of official ceremony, especially when neither of them knew what the future held. Frederic had a lot of adjustment ahead of him. Preparing for a sightless future. And Piper needed to figure out what she wanted to do with her life now that she'd parted ways with French cooking. She and Mrs. Lesner had talked about maybe opening a small bisro in Paris specializing in classic comfort food. There would be plenty of expatriates looking for a home-cooked meal.

One thing she was certain of, though, was that Frederic owned her heart and that, when the time came, she would be thrilled to make their commitment legal. In the meantime, she was more than happy with being his makeshift bride.

They "married" themselves in the field behind the abbey. Frederic's idea. "I want to watch you walk down the aisle," he said. "In case..." He didn't need to finish his reason why.

Frederic held her hands in his. "I promise to never push you away again," he said. "I will accept your help, and I will never let you lose yourself."

"And I promise to never act out of obligation," Piper replied. "Whatever happens in the future, we will face it together."

She smiled a watery smile at the man she planned on loving forever. Funny how things worked out. She came to Paris with one dream and found another. One that was far better. As for the future...they would simply have to figure it out as they went along. Time was theirs to make what they wanted. So long as she and Frederic stood together, they would be fine. More than fine. She'd be happier than she'd ever imagined.

And to think it all started with Ana's missing portrait.

"Oh, no!" The exclamation burst from her mouth, disrupting the moment and turning Frederic pale.

"What's wrong, love?"

"I never called Patience. With everything going on between the two of us… It's been almost two weeks since I've talked to her." Her sister hadn't called her, either, a point she would make if Patience complained. "She has no idea what's going on." She held out her hand. "Can I borrow your cell phone?"

"Married for two minutes, and already you are pushing me aside for your sister? I have not even kissed the bride."

Piper kissed him long and slow, a promise of what was to come. When they finally broke apart, she rested her forehead against his. "That better?"

"Perfect."

"Good. Give me your phone." She was grinning from ear to ear. "Patience! Did I wake you? I've got good news and I've got more good news. The good news is we found Ana's portrait and the owner's willing to talk to Stuart about selling." Legs bouncing, she waited impatiently for her sister to relay the news. Frederic laughed and kissed her forehead.

Finally, Patience's voice came back on the line. "You said there's more good news. What is it?"

"I got married!" she exclaimed.

And, holding her husband's hand, she filled her sister in on her happy ending.

Christmas Day

Ana knew something was up from all the looks Patience and her nephew exchanged during Christmas dinner. Of course, she assumed they planned to announce their engagement, so when Stuart asked her to close her eyes, she was confused.

"Why do I have to close my eyes?" she asked him. "We've already opened the gifts."

Stuart gave her one of his annoying smirks, the one he reserved for when he had a secret. "Maybe not. Maybe there's a surprise present."

Goodness, how could there be more gifts? You could barely move around the room as it was, what with the tree and all the presents.

A slender arm wrapped around her shoulders. It was Patience, her nephew's partner in crime. "Please, Ana. I promise you won't be disappointed."

"Oh, all right." She couldn't say no to that girl if she tried.

Although she should have pointed out that no matter what the surprise, she couldn't possibly be disappointed. Certainly not after such a wonderful Christmas celebration. In addition to Patience and Stuart, Patience's sister was visiting from France along with her boyfriend. *Boyfriend*, Ana chuckled. Frederic was no boy. Her Nigel would have said *sa grande passion*, the way the two of them lit up whenever the other entered the room. But then, he would use the same phrase for Stuart and Patience as well.

How wonderful it had been to spend the day surrounded by love. To see the people she loved in love. It thrilled her to know that while she had lost her chance, others had not. She ran her hand over the cat nestled in her lap. Sweet Nigel. He'd be thrilled, too. He used to say it was love that gave his art life. For a man who claimed to be a rebel, he was a hopeless romantic.

"Okay, *babushka*. Open your eyes."

No… It couldn't… Ana's heart leaped to her throat. "How…?" Her legs were shaking so hard she was afraid they wouldn't hold her.

Patience was at her elbow, supporting her "Piper and Frederic tracked her down in England," she said.

"Turns out a man named Gaspard Theroux held out on Grandpa Theodore," Stuart told her "He never told him that he owned one of Nigel' works."

"Dear sweet Gaspard. He believed in Nigel's talent before anyone else." She ran her trembling fingers across her younger self, along the brush-strokes she remembered so well. Nigel painted with such vitality, such passion. "He was so proud of this work."

Time turned backward, and she was in Paris, stretched across the velvet settee. "Don't move, *mon amour*. The light on your skin is perfect. I want the whole world to see you the way I do."

She would have lain in place forever if that's what he needed.

A tear ran down her cheek. "Please don't cry," Patience said.

The dear girl didn't understand. These were happy tears. Nigel's work survived. In spite of all Theodore's efforts to erase it, proof of their love lived on.

Leaving the tears to fall, she turned to Piper and Frederic. "Thank you."

"No," Piper said. "Thank you. If not for your painting, Frederic and I would still be…"

"The two loneliest people in Paris," Frederic supplied, pressing a kiss to her forehead. "Your Nigel brought us together."

He would have been so glad to know that. Ana turned back to the portrait. The years hadn't diminished its strength. She could still feel the emotion in every stroke. *I miss you so much, my darling.*

"We'll be together soon enough, mon amour."

In the meantime, she would celebrate. She would bask in the love shared by the young people around her, and give thanks for the happy endings she knew would be theirs.

With Nigel close by. "This moment calls for a celebration," she said. "*Lapushka*, go get some champagne from the wine cellar. And you, my furry rascal..." Reaching down, she scooped up the cat she'd unceremoniously dumped when she stood up. "Let us toast to your namesake. And to happy endings."

It was exactly what Nigel would have wanted.

* * * * *

MIL